STUCK FAST IN YESTERDAY

STUCK FAST IN YESTERDAY
Heather Kellerhals-Stewart

A Groundwood Book
Douglas & McIntyre
Vancouver/Toronto

Douglas & McIntyre Ltd.
1615 Venables Street
Vancouver, British Columbia.

Canadian Cataloguing in Publication Data
Kellerhals-Stewart, Heather, 1937-
   Stuck fast in yesterday

ISBN 0-88899-024-3

I. Title.
PS8571.E44S78   jC813′.54   C83-098620-0
PZ7.K44St

Cover art by Graham Bardell
Design by Maher and Murtagh
Printed and bound in Canada by D.W. Friesen & Sons Ltd.

To my mother, Ruth, and her parents,
Thomasina Maude and Benjamin Kilbourn.

Do diddle di do,
Poor Jim Jay
Got stuck fast
In Yesterday.

Walter de la Mare

1

Museum Sunday Blues

Jennifer squished her nose against the window. The rain running in rivers down the outside seemed to be streaking across her own face. "Keep falling, rain—in buckets, in bathtubs for all I care, so long as you do my crying for me. I'm feeling too cross to cry."

Jennifer squeezed the four quarters that she had in her pocket, then popped one into her mouth and bit on it. "Now I'll be crawling with creepy germs," she thought.

Those four pieces of silver were supposed to have taken her to see the special Sunday matinee showing of the "Black Stallion," but instead . . .

"It'll be off by next week," Jennifer yelled at her mother when the idea of a museum visit had first been suggested.

"And you know how horse-crazy Shann is and I triple-promised her we'd go to the movie together."

"The Royal Ontario Museum has a special photographic exhibit going on," her mother persevered. "You know how keen your father is about photography. Besides, we so seldom do anything as a family nowadays and Aunty Isabel has invited us afterwards to an early supper."

So here she was at the museum, wearing a skirt and her coat with the scratchy collar. The twenty-five cent pieces felt all sweaty inside her hand. Jennifer pressed her face against the window again, watching the fog as it began to thread tentacle-like through the tree branches. It writhed against the window, searching for a crack.

"I'd let you in if I could," Jennifer whispered, " and

then we would go rolling down the corridor together and trip up that museum guard or better still, I'd sneak away someplace with you."

"Jennifer . . . where . . . oh, there you are!" her father's voice boomed out.

Jennifer appeared from the alcove where she had taken refuge. "I've been waiting here for ages."

"What on earth have you smudged all across your face Jennifer? And look at your white blouse. Have you been leaning against something dirty?"

"I guess I was leaning on the window in there. It's not my fault the museum has such filthy windows," she added.

Her father coughed. "I have had quite enough of your irritable talk for one day, young lady. Now if you don't mind I should like to look, undisturbed, at these old photographs."

Jennifer clamped down on her tongue. When her father spoke in such formal tones it usually meant a storm was smouldering somewhere. She clumped along behind her parents with a sour expression on her face, wishing that her legs didn't look like skinny stilts sticking out from her skirt, wishing that she wasn't so incredibly ugly anyhow, but most of all wishing that she could be anywhere except inside a boring museum, tagging after two parents.

At the entrance to the special exhibit a sign announced, "Around the Year in Photographs, Circa 1900," and standing near the sign was a life-sized model of a photographer bent over an old-fashioned camera. As Jennifer walked past she aimed an imaginary kick at his backside. The photographer's camera was pointed towards a family portrait that had also been blown up to life-size. Jennifer stared at the prissy-looking kids in the picture. "I bet you never had much fun in those old-fashioned clothes."

As Jennifer said this, the girl in the photograph shook her head ever so slightly. Or did she? Jennifer tried to step back for a better look, but her feet refused to budge. Now all the eyes in the photograph were turning to stare at her.

"Jennifer, try and keep up so we won't become separated," her father called back.

Jennifer wrenched herself free from the mocking faces. What a dummy she was, letting her imagination run away till she was all tied up in knots! They always used special effects in these exhibits, such as recorded music and sounds to make you think you were deep down in the ocean or floating up in space. Or you could go through an old house and actually hear water boiling on the stove and smell cookies baking in the oven. That's all it was—just a trick.

From curiosity Jennifer reached out to touch the surface of the picture, but an arm grabbed hers. "Can't you read the notice, kid? Do not touch the photographs. I'm forever wiping off finger-prints around here. Grease, peanut butter, plain old dirt, you name it!"

Jennifer practically fell over backwards. It was the museum guard she knew from previous visits. He was always following kids around and eyeing them suspiciously, especially if they had no adults along. And now, oh groan! There was her father coming back to retrieve her.

"Jennifer, if you can't keep up, you will simply have to walk ahead of us."

"What does he think I am, a little two year old or something?" Jennifer stomped off around the exhibit, making sure she was well in front of her parents.

However, the photographs were set up in such a way that even the most uninterested person could hardly fail to see something. Down rows, around corners, into deadends she wandered; it was like a maze. Every now and then Jennifer caught herself looking at a picture. "Trust those museum types for being so sneaky," she grumbled. "Bet I'll take ages to find my way out."

Jennifer swung around to look for directions and almost bumped into one of the photographs. A caption underneath it read, 'Seen and Not Heard Children—First Day at School.' Jennifer repeated the words out loud. "Seen and not heard . . . if you ask me that's a funny way of describing a bunch of kids who had to shut up all the time.'' Seen and Not Heard . . . Seen and Not Heard . . . the words were doing a wobbly dance in front of her eyes as if they were struggling to keep in time with some invisible conductor. At the same time the figures in the photograph seemed to be changing and growing upwards. Jennifer looked away to rest her eyes.

But now other figures, behind, all around her, were shooting up and straining to burst out of their picture frames.

"I caught a glimpse of her ahead of us," came her father's voice from somewhere deep in the maze of photographs. "I expect she'll find her own way out."

Jennifer began to walk very quickly, past photographs of children playing outside or caught in some stiff indoor pose, past photographs taken in winter and summer, until without warning she found herself back with her parents. "I've been around this whole exhibit and you've barely moved," Jennifer complained.

Her father glanced at his watch. "I tell you what. You run off and look at something else for a while. Just be sure you are back here in half an hour so we won't be late for supper."

"What a waste of time that was!" Jennifer grumbled, hurrying off. "Maybe now I can look at something interesting like the dinosaurs or Egyptian mummies." She made a face at the model of the old-fashioned photographer standing guard at the entrance to the exhibit. Her coat must have brushed against the stand, because the photographer seemed to turn, and instead of looking at the family portrait he was staring after Jennifer as she ran down the length of the museum hall. Several old-fashioned dolls, sitting ever so primly inside their glass cases, stared disapprovingly at the creature hurtling past them.

"No runn-ing," the museum guard hollered after her. "Hey kid, didn't you hear me say no running."

But Jennifer was already hopping down some steps. "I can't stop," she thought to herself. "I'm in too much trouble already."

Close behind Jennifer and keeping in time with the thumping of her heart, was the heavy clump, clump, clump of the guard's footsteps. He was gaining ground! "Where can I hide?" Jennifer kept asking herself. "Where? The guard must know every little corner of this building. And if I don't get a brainwave pretty soon . . . "

Jennifer ducked around a corner and into an alcove, pressing herself tightly against the wall. The guard's footsteps flashed past her hiding place. "He'll be back," Jennifer thought, "but at least I have a head start on him. And with luck maybe I can hide myself in the crowds of people."

Jennifer stepped out from the alcove, but at that very moment the guard swung around in his tracks. "All right, stay where you are, kid. We've got a few things to talk about, you and me."

Jennifer didn't wait to hear what they were. She was already running back down the hallway, past the Egyptian mummies who stared shrunken-eyed at this noisy intruder, around several more corners . . . Where were the usual Sunday crowds when she needed them most? A heavy-looking door appeared ahead of her. "I don't remember any door being here." A second later she was forced to an abrupt halt beneath a sign which read, "No admittance. Museum Staff Only."

What now? That great, hulking door was blocking the way ahead. Jennifer looked around for another escape route. There was absolutely nothing, not even a window to climb through. Suddenly she heard the guard's footsteps coming around the corner at the end of the hall. She was trapped!

Without thinking Jennifer grabbed the doorknob, pulled as hard as her shaking hands would allow and felt the door opening. A rush of damp, unpleasant air slipped across Jennifer's face, making her hesitate for a moment, but the guard was close behind. And if he saw the open door . . .

Jennifer stepped across the threshold and as she turned

to pull the door after her discovered it was already swinging shut. With a sharp "click" both the light and sounds from outside were cut off. "I'm safe," she panted. "At least I hope I am."

The darkness snatched up the sound of Jennifer's voice and swung it to the shadows beyond. Any moment now the guard might burst through the door and then what? At last Jennifer had to take a breath. It came out in a long, quavery sigh. The silence hung around her like a thick blanket, waiting. Where was that guard anyhow? How come she couldn't hear him? "If you think it's smart to lurk outside there waiting for me, you're in for a big surprise. I'm not walking into any trap."

Jennifer was shocked by the sound of her own voice. If only it wasn't so completely black. Everything seemed worse when you couldn't see to the end of your own nose. Jennifer had not moved since the door had slammed shut behind her. Presuming there must be a light switch near it, she began moving her hands over the wall.

"The door was right her a minute ago. I'm positive. After all, I came through it to get in here!"

For a moment Jennifer felt she was suffocating and she sank down on her hands and knees groping blindly for a keyhole, a knob, a crack of light . . . There wasn't the slightest hint of a door anywhere—only a cold, concrete wall that had a dank, underground sort of smell to it. Jennifer pressed her ear against the wall, but listening only seemed to make her more aware of the tomb-like atmosphere of the place. No muffled voices, footsteps or distant swish of traffic softened the silence; there was just the sound of her own breathing becoming louder and more frightened.

"I bet you that guard is trying to give me a good scare. Well, if he thinks he can teach me a lesson this way . . . "

For a few seconds the welcome feeling of anger swept away Jennifer's fear, allowing her to notice a glimmer of light in a far corner of the room. It flickered once or twice, went out completely and then revived again. "There must be someone working over there," she decided, "and perhaps another door too."

Jennifer began feeling her way towards the far side of the room. Everywhere she turned there were boxes. The place was probably a gigantic storeroom or workshop. Once Jennifer touched what felt like a pile of bones and she shivered and jerked away. "Only old dinosaur bones waiting to be put together," she told herself. As she drew closer to the light she could make out the shapes of some old fashioned machines. In the wavering light they cast grotesque shadows across the floor and took on strange shapes like some ghostly collection of prehistoric monsters. The jagged teeth of one of them leapt out from the darkness to slash across her leg. "Ouch!"

While Jennifer was bending over to rub her shin, she heard a soft, swishing sound as if something were being dragged across the floor.

"Is . . . is anyone there?" Jennifer whispered.

The rustling stopped abruptly, but Jennifer heard the echo of a laugh that was swallowed up in the shadows. After listening and hearing nothing more than her own heartbeat Jennifer began inching her way towards the pale circle cast by the light. An old threshing machine was blocking the way. Rather than going around it Jennifer crawled underneath where she could remain hidden from view. Brushing aside the dust-laden cobwebs that were hanging from the bottom she was finally able to look out on the other side.

Jennifer whistled silently. The light was coming from an old fashioned gas street lamp. But what was sitting underneath the light interested her even more. It was a large chest with the lid hanging open. If only she were close enough to see inside!

She watched and waited. Nothing moved except the gas lamp which occasionally flickered and then flared up again.

13

"I can't stay under here forever," Jennifer muttered to herself. "Besides, there might be something useful in that chest."

Silently, like the shadows around her, Jennifer slipped towards the chest and leaned over. "Nothing but old clothes!" she breathed out. Dust rose up as she rumpled through the contents. "Achoo!" Jennifer swung round in alarm after she had sneezed, half expecting a door to burst open or a voice to call out. But nothing happened. When she reached back into the chest her fingers came to rest on something soft and furry. Jennifer pulled the thing out. It was a hand muff which looked strangely familiar.

Jennifer rummaged through the chest looking for more things. A hat with ribbons came flying out, followed by a skirt and sailor style blouse, black stockings and a pair of pointed boots. "Might as well have some fun trying them on," Jennifer thought, "and maybe I can disguise myself." The idea of escaping under the very nose of the museum guard pleased her no end.

As she threw off her own coat, the four quarters that had been in one pocket bounced out and rolled along the floor. Jennifer managed to grab a single coin before it vanished into the darkness with the others. "I'll look for them later," she decided. "Right now I want to try on these clothes."

The skirt and blouse fit perfectly. And so did the hat. While she was bending down to pull on the boots a voice whispered from out of the shadows. "How charming you look now. No . . . don't spoil the picture by moving away."

There was a rustling among the shadows, something was slowly taking shape and moving towards her. The figure became clearer. It looked exactly like the model standing outside the photographic exhibit. No, that wasn't possible!

"But it is him!" Jennifer gasped.

The old-fashioned photographer, draped in a black cloak and carrying the same camera from the museum, was only an arm's length away from her now. "What a delightful addition you will be to my collection. I fancy you can be made into a perfect 'seen and not heard' child, given time . . . time . . . time . . ."

As the words echoed like a gigantic clock over Jennifer's head, she backed away and stumbled against the gas lamp. It flickered once and slowly began to dim. While there was still a glimmer of light remaining, Jennifer scrambled to the top of the threshing machine. Was he following? She had no time to look back. There was a sudden rumbling sound and the metal under Jennifer's feet began to vibrate. Struggling to keep her balance she slipped onto the tongue of the threshing machine and found to her horror that she was being dragged towards a set of terrible slashing teeth. Before Jennifer could cry out she was somehow past them and inside the metal monster, spiralling down into the roaring darkness. Then a sudden blast of air came and light so blinding that Jennifer could feel the throb of it behind her clenched eyes. She felt herself being catapulted outwards. Suddenly she was sinking into something soft, yet scratchy feeling.

2
Backwards in Time

The noise stopped and through the quietness a bird's song drifted reassuringly. Although Jennifer could feel a hand resting on her forehead, it seemed to be from across a vast distance. She struggled to open her eyes, but could not. And then a girl's voice was reaching out, drawing her back to life. "She's not dead, Benjamin. I can feel her breath on my hand."

"Of course she isn't dead, Thomasina," a boy's voice interrupted. "Whatever put that strange notion into your head? People don't die on top of straw stacks in the middle of a field, silly. She is only asleep."

Jennifer felt a soothing breeze run across her closed eyes. Wherever she was it wasn't raining or dark anymore; in fact the sun felt warm on her forehead.

"She might have taken a chill overnight and then pneumonia," the girl's voice insisted, " so don't call me silly. Isn't she pretty though, Benjamin?"

Jennifer heard the other voice drawing closer. "How would I know if she is pretty or not? I don't care a pin for girls."

Silence. Jennifer struggled to move her lips. What she wanted to tell them was, "I can hear every word you're saying." But no sound came from her mouth.

The boy's voice continued. "There is something very strange about this girl, Thom. I'm not exactly sure what it is. Look at her hair; it's like stubble in the fields. And what's more, the stockings she is wearing are all torn and she has no shoes either."

Once again, Jennifer felt the girl's hand brushing across her face.

"Benjamin, come here, quickly. I feel her eyelids moving. At least I think I did."

And she was right. Jennifer was opening her eyes so she could tell these two kids who were bending over her, practically breathing into her face, to run off and mind their own business. What Jennifer saw, however, caused her to clamp her eyes shut again. Though she couldn't understand how it was remotely possible, they were those children from the family portrait in the museum! Jennifer tried to think back. The photographer's camera had been pointing towards the picture and the figures had been blown up to life size to make them look more real. With a sudden start, Jennifer remembered how the girl had seemed to nod her head ever so slightly. Then all the other eyes in the picture had turned to stare at her.

Jennifer sat up with her eyes wide open. No, it wasn't all a dream. The girl was still standing there, watching her. If it wasn't a dream, then where was she? "Oh, no!" Jennifer put both hands to her head.

The sensation of spinning through space, beyond the reach of familiar planets, crushed down on her. Where was she going? How could she stop this dizzying spiral? Jennifer tried to steady herself, to stop the terrible throbbing in her ears. Her fingernails bit into the palm of one hand, curling against something hard and real—a single coin. Somehow she had managed to hold onto the twenty-five cent piece. The throbbing gradually stopped and she could hear voices again.

"Are you all right?" the boy was saying. "My name is Benjamin and this is my sister, Thomasina."

"Oh, don't bother with that long-drawn-out name Thomasina. I'd rather be Thom . ... What's your name? Do you live near here? I haven't seen you at school . . . "

Realizing that she didn't have a speedy answer to all these questions, Jennifer rolled onto her stomach with her hands clasped behind her head. "Leave me alone. Can't you see I've got too rotten a headache to be answering a whole pile of questions?"

Benjamin was nudging his sister. "You see, Thomasina—you have gone and offended her with all your questions."

Glancing over her shoulder, Jennifer could see that Benjamin was standing on the very edge of the straw stack. With all her strength she kicked back with both legs. Benjamin was bowled over and began to slide slowly, feet first, over the edge of the stack. Thom peeked over the edge, lost her footing and fell over too.

As fast as she could, Jennifer sat up and slid down the opposite side of the straw stack. Underneath was a cave-like hollow. Jennifer crawled in and pulled some straw over the opening. A few minutes later she heard Thom shouting from the top. "She isn't up here. Why don't you go look around the other stacks, Benjamin?"

"Why should I be bothered looking for such a tomboy," Benjamin grumbled. "She can stay hidden for all I care."

"Good!" thought Jennifer. For the moment she had managed to escape those kids with their pestering questions. The important thing now was to think up a convincing story, because nobody would believe the real one, not in a thousand years. Jennifer shook her head. The more she thought about it, the more confused she felt. What was the real story? What was she doing here with two old-fashioned kids? She hadn't wanted to go anywhere; all she wanted was to get away from that boring photographic exhibit in the museum. The photographer! Jennifer suddenly remembered his words. "What a delightful addition you will be to my collection" and "I fancy you can be made into a perfect seen and not heard child." Jennifer shivered. Suppose the whole business was a scheme of his . . . Suppose he had transported her back in time as a sort of prisoner . . .

"I don't know who or what you are muttering about, but I'm here." Thomasina's face appeared through the straw, grinning like a cheshire cat. "Do you mind if I come in?"

"I suppose not."

"You see I thought we might have a peaceful chat without that bossy brother of mine around. Just as I reached the top of the straw stack again I saw the tail end of you disappearing in here. Oh the way you knocked my brother down—that was splendid! Most of the girls I know won't do anything risky, not even run. I love running, I do. It's as if I am singing my own self along with the wind whistling past my ears and through my teeth . . . if you know what I mean." She glanced shyly over at Jennifer. "Here I am talking about myself and I don't even know your name!"

Jennifer hesitated and frowned. That tightly coiled up part inside her that was always spitting out something mean or sarcastic was up to its usual tricks. She felt like saying, "So what?" But she had never had a real friend, the kind you could feel relaxed with and who wouldn't laugh at you or how you looked, even if you felt dumb. And if ever she needed a friend, it was now.

Thom was still waiting for Jennifer to reply, but all traces of the initial smile had vanished from her face. "You certainly do look cross. And I know it's because of something foolish I said. Everyone is always saying I talk too much . . . oh dear!"

"Wait a minute, it isn't your fault if I'm cross. Anyhow, sometimes I look grouchy when I'm really not." Suddenly Jennifer felt ashamed. For some reason she felt like spilling the whole story out to this strange, persistent kid. "I've come such a long way," Jennifer heard herself saying. "You see I left home very suddenly and it may not be that easy going back . . . Oh, and my name is Jennifer."

Thomasina swallowed hard. "You mean you ran away

from home and you have no place to stay? Then of course you must come home with us. Were they dreadfully cruel to you? My father is a doctor and he is always looking after children who have been whipped too hard or had their ears boxed. Do you hurt anywhere in particular?''

If Thomasina hadn't looked so genuinely worried, Jennifer would have burst out laughing. ''No, no, they didn't beat me up at home or anything like that. But you are right about one thing, I don't have any place to stay.''

''Thom-a-sin-a!'' Benjamin's voice was very close. ''Wherever are you? Don't tell me she has gone and hidden too. Thom-a-sin-a!''

Thom nudged aside a few wisps of straw to reveal Benjamin or at least his legs, standing only a few inches away from the straw stack. She whispered something to Jennifer and with a shriek the two of them dove at his ankles. Down he went, like a sapling bending before the wind. A few minutes later he was picking straw of his breeches and complaining bitterly about tomboys.

''At least they know how to build tree forts,'' Thomasina reminded him.

''Not worth it, not for one minute, especially when they are getting me into trouble again by making us late for supper. Now where has that lazy beast gone? Black Beauty . . . Black Beauty,'' he whistled. A pony was standing beside one of the straw stacks leisurely pulling out mouthfuls of straw.

''You mean we are going to ride in that?'' Jennifer was pointing towards a flimsy-looking cart hitched to Black Beauty.

''Nobody says you have to,'' Benjamin replied. ''Is something wrong with our pony and cart?''

''Uh, nothing really. You see I live in the city and . . . ''

''You have horses there, just the same as us, don't you?''

''But I don't have my own pony and cart, that's all I meant.''

20

Benjamin nudged his sister. "Did you tell her that she could come home with us?"

Jennifer heard Thom whispering. "Sssh, don't talk so loudly, Benjamin. You never gave me a chance to tell you. She has run away from home."

Benjamin groaned. "Trust you, Thomasina! You are always finding helpless creatures, but this is going one step too far. What will Father and Mother say? How do we know she isn't a tramp or a gypsy or . . . or, anything? She behaves so strangely and just listen to her speech."

"Not so loud, Benjamin, she can hear you."

"Perhaps it will do her some good then. Come on Black Beauty, let's be off home."

Having little other choice Jennifer climbed into the cart behind the other two. For the first time she had a chance to look at her surroundings. The afternoon sun was reflected from the roofs of what appeared to be a small town lying some distance across the fields. Curls of smoke were rising up from the houses, turning into golden fountains through which flocks of birds darted after invisible insects. Jennifer blinked at the brilliance of it all. The day had an indescribably end-of-summer feeling about it that was too golden to last. Once or twice she squeezed the twenty-five cent piece in her hand to make sure she was not dreaming. As the cart bumped across the fields and onto the gravel road Jennifer kept glancing backwards. Occasionally a wagon or buggy passed going the other way, but that was all. Yet an uneasy feeling that they were being followed hung over Jennifer until the cart reached the outskirts of town. Then, without warning, Black Beauty shot around a corner and up a dirt lane leading towards a brick house. Jennifer found herself sitting on the bottom of the cart, her hat floating somewhere behind in the clouds of dust.

"He always does that when he smells home," Benjamin chuckled as he watched Jennifer. "Gave you a scare, I warrant."

"Not a bit! It takes more than a stubborn pony and a

half-asleep driver to scare me.'' Jennifer stared straight at Benjamin until he turned away.

Thom squeezed Jennifer's hand. "Now don't worry. Mother and Father will be delighted to see you.''

"And what about Josephine!'' Benjamin interrupted. "Won't she be enchanted to see another child standing on her kitchen steps. The two of you look like a pair of scarecrows standing there; especially when you stick out your tongue like that, little Miss Thomasina.''

"THOMASINA! BENJAMIN!'' Josephine had just appeared on the kitchen porch and was staring through her wire-rimmed glasses at the three straw-covered figures standing in front of her. "Who may I ask is your companion? Doesn't she have any shoes?''

Thomasina motioned to Jennifer to keep quiet. "We met Jennifer here while we were out for a drive with Black Beauty. Because she had to run away from home and can't go back right away, I thought perhaps . . . well she ought to stay with us.''

Josephine stared down at Jennifer. "What an uncommonly strange-looking girl! Where did you pick up those clothes, child? I haven't seen a blouse like that for years.''

"My name is Jennifer, not child. And I'm only wearing these old-fashioned clothes because my own got left behind. It's not my fault.'' And it's none of your business, Jennifer would like to have added, but she had already said too much. If she didn't watch her tongue they would begin to suspect she wasn't telling the truth and then there would be trouble.

Josephine looked at the three children for what seemed like an eternity. Finally . . . "So be it, Thomasina. Under these circumstances I have little choice but to ask Jennifer in for supper. However, I must discuss the matter with your parents later on. Now I shall thank you three to march straight over to that pump before you so much as set one foot inside my kitchen. Cleanliness is next to Godliness,'' she said with a glance heavenwards and disappeared into the house.

"Who is she?" Jennifer managed to stutter out between giggles.

Thomasina was jumping around frantically. "Jennifer—ssh! Josephine is our housekeeper, but she doesn't just keep it, she rules it. If she sees you laughing she will drag us by our hair to the pump and scrub us clean herself."

Benjamin grabbed his sister's shoulder and propelled her towards the pump. "I'm not getting into trouble with Josephine again because of you two girls." He marched back to Jennifer and caught her by the wrist.

"I can walk to the pump without any boy's help, thank you very much."

Benjamin stared at Jennifer for a moment before letting go of her arm. He walked back to the pump where Thomasina was busily splashing water over her hands and face. "She is a real terror, that one. Wait until Josephine meets her close up. I expect we shall see fireworks then."

Jennifer walked up and took her place beside the other two. Washing at a hand pump wasn't so bad, she decided, especially when you felt itchy all over from bits of straw. Jennifer let the cold water run down her cheeks and trickle in icy circles around the back of her neck. Everything was so different—even the way people washed here. She would have to be on guard against saying things that sounded out of place. Thom was more or less okay, but the boy—yech! If he was any indication of what the adults were like, things were going to be rough.

Jennifer was still shaking the stray drops of water from her hair when Josephine reappeared on the kitchen porch. "Supper is ready," she announced.

Jennifer didn't protest when Thom took her arm going into Josephine's kitchen domain; in fact it felt definitely reassuring. The smell of freshly baked cinnamon muffins was rising up from the wood stove and spreading into every corner of the room. Less inviting, though, was the smell rising up from a tureen of soup sitting on a table set for the three of them.

"Your parents are taking tea in the parlour with some guests," Josephine announced.

"And not having your terrible food," Thomasina muttered under her breath.

Josephine began ladling some soup into three bowls where she had already placed three sausages. As Jennifer leaned over her bowl the sausage looked like a fat frog peeking through the surface.

"I'm supposed to eat that!" Jennifer almost said out loud. Luckily Thom had read her thoughts in time and catching hold of Jennifer's hand directed it towards a ledge under the table where an assortment of dried-up food bits was already hiding. The two of them grinned in secret understanding.

Across the table Benjamin was sitting with his eyes closed in preparation for the blessing. "Thank you for the food we eat . . . may the Lord make us truly thankful. Aaa-men."

Josephine had barely closed her mouth over the resounding "Amen," when Thomasina plunged her fork into the sausage. With a tiny squeal the grease whistled up into the air, spraying Josephine who was standing over the table. Jennifer started giggling and choked on a crust of bread until the tears were streaming down her face.

Josephine exploded. "Thomasina, I have told you countless times how to manage a knife and fork. We do not plunge a fork into food as if it were something to be butchered. Manners maketh the Man, Thomasina."

"Who wants to be a man!" Thom complained under her breath to Jennifer.

"All right, my fine young ladies—there will be no cinnamon muffins for you this evening."

For several minutes the only sound was the clink of their spoons against the soup bowls. Jennifer jumped when a piece of wood in the stove suddenly popped and split open. Once or twice she caught Benjamin staring at her with a puzzled expression on his face. It made her cross. Finally

Josephine took away the soup bowls. Thomasina, who had been fidgeting around in her chair for the last five minutes, burst up from the table.

"Wait!" Josephine ordered. "Show me your face." She mopped an invisible speck of soup from Thom's face, then made a move towards Jennifer.

"Don't touch me with that dish water rag!" Jennifer jumped up from the table.

Josephine turned a formidable shade of red.

"I don't blame you, Jennifer, but it's no use protesting," Benjamin whispered as he went by.

"I didn't ask for your advice," Jennifer hissed.

The commotion from the kitchen brought the grownups hurrying to the door.

"What is all the fuss about?" asked Father. "Oh, we have a visitor, I see."

Josephine sniffed. "A street urchin whom Thomasina brought home!"

From what seemed an enormous height, Father gazed down upon Jennifer. She suddenly felt very small and shabby, standing there with no shoes, torn stockings and a blouse with loose threads hanging from the sleeves. His eyes from under bushy brows seemed to be looking right through her.

Thom came to the rescue. "Jennifer had to run away from home, Father. But it wasn't her fault—I'm positive. We just happened to meet her when we were out with Black Beauty, otherwise I don't know what would have happened. She has no place to stay or . . ."

"You poor child!" Mother broke in, giving Jennifer a hug. "Of course she may stay with us, Thomasina, until we are able to find out something about her own home. We won't talk about it any more while we have guests. You may take Jennifer up to your room and see if any of your clothes will fit her." She turned to Josephine. "Do make sure the two of them have a good wash before going upstairs, Josephine." And more quietly she added so Jennifer could scarcely hear, "We ought to wash the child's hair and throw away the old clothes. Who knows where she comes from!"

Josephine shook her head. "It will come to no good, mark my words."

"Now, Josephine," Father said, "I know having another child makes extra work for you, but it will only be temporary until we find some better solution. None of us would wish to turn away an unfortunate child, I'm sure."

Later on as Jennifer followed Thomasina down the long hallway past the parlour door, she could hear scraps of the grownup's conversation.

"Something strange about that child," Father's voice was saying, "difficult to describe . . . almost other worldly . . ."

"It's more than Christian of you, Maude and Timothy, to take in a homeless waif."

"But we could never turn a child away . . ."

"So many runaways . . . what is this world coming to?"

"We shall have to report the child as missing, though I fear we shall hear nothing . . ." Jennifer lost the end of Father's sentence as she and Thom climbed the stairway at the end of the hall.

"Here we are," Thom announced at the top of the stairs. "This is my room on the right, Benjamin's is over there and the big bedroom belongs to Mother and Father."

"Where's the bathroom?"

"The what?"

"The bathroom. You know . . . like if I want to take a bath or have to get up in the middle of the night to pee."

"Oh, I see what you mean! I keep forgetting you are from the city." Thomasina looked a bit alarmed. "Well, most of the time we have baths on Saturday nights so as to be all clean for Sunday church or perhaps when we are sick with a high fever. Did you see our big tub hanging beside the kitchen stove? And if you have to get up in the middle of the night for . . . um . . . a visit, there is a pot under the bed." Thom gulped and went on. "But I'd rather you go down to the woodshed. We're lucky. Most people only have an outhouse way back of the house which is freezing in winter.''

"I bet!" Jennifer agreed under her breath. Was she ever going to have to watch what she said. Anyhow it was a relief to be away from the grownups. Around Thom she felt more comfortable, even when they were being quiet.

While Thomasina was rummaging through her drawers for extra clothes, Jennifer wandered around the room. Like her own bedroom at home every nook and cranny was filled with something—bird feathers, rocks, pictures of animals, a turtle shell, the skeleton of a mouse gathering dust on a shelf . . . However, the room was much smaller and simpler than hers; colder too, judging by the heavy quilt spread across the bed. Jennifer reached out to touch the stovepipe that ran up through the floor, then jerked her hand back. It was surprisingly hot.

Thomasina had been watching her. "What's your house like?" she asked suddenly. "You haven't told me very much. You said it's in the city somewhere, but it doesn't sound like my grandparents' house in Toronto.''

Was Thom looking at here suspiciously or was she only imagining it? "Um . . . well what do you want to know?"

"Oh, never mind. You can tell me some other time when you aren't so tired. Houses aren't that fascinating anyhow. Did you have to walk a long way today?'' Thom asked abruptly.

"Not too far," Jennifer replied truthfully. "I got a ride most of the way.''

Thomasina handed her something. "Here, better put this on before Josephine starts nagging us about going to bed. It's still too long for me so probably it will be about right for you.''

Jennifer undressed quickly and pulled the nightgown over her head. Help! She would smother in it or drown in all the folds. Thomasina was sitting on the edge of the bed laughing her head off. "What's so funny?"

"You are. You look terribly long-suffering."

"Maybe I am!" Jennifer didn't add that most of the time she would rather drop dead than wear anything but pyjamas to bed. She thought of the disgusting nightie that her mother had bought once and the awful fight they had over it. "I don't care if they look more feminine than pyjamas. I hate nighties," she had said. Thinking about home brought Jennifer back down to earth. What had happened to her resolve to be more cautious? "I guess if you have nothing else for me to wear it'll do, but at least you could stop laughing."

For a long time they lay awake in bed talking. Thom finally dozed off in the middle of a sentence, tried several times to continue, then gave up and fell into a deep sleep. Mother and Father said good-bye to their guests and came upstairs. Gradually the house grew still. But Jennifer tossed and turned in bed, trying to find a comfortable position. The nightgown kept twisting around her ankles or climbing into folds around her knees.

She began to count the half and quarter hours as the grandfather clock in the hall chimed through the darkness. Was it the same time at home, she wondered or had she lost all track of time? Would they be back yet from supper at Aunty Isabel's? She thought of the yummy, double-decked sandwiches that Aunty Isabel always made for her. Would they be wondering where she was and worrying? Ten-thirty . . . eleven . . . eleven-fifteen . . . She must have dropped off to sleep, but something woke her again—an object falling, a door closing? She couldn't say. The same panicky feeling that had gripped her on the road and stayed with her almost to the house grew in her chest. She looked around the room. The moonlight was streaming in through the window and glancing off a photograph hung above Thomasina's chest of drawers. As she watched, the figures in the photo started to expand until they seemed about to burst from the frame. Then as rapidly as they had grown they shrank back into the picture. The old-fashioned photographer! The image of his figure in the museum sprang into Jennifer's mind. She knew now. How could she have ever thought otherwise! Like his own photographs he could leap across time and somewhere out there he was watching and waiting . . . He had time . . . the clock in the hall was striking again. Jennifer lost count. She ducked under the sheets and pulled the quilt over her head to block out the sound. Her fingers brushed against the twenty-five cent piece that she had put under the pillow for safekeeping. Touching something familiar reminded her that Thom was still there too. She stretched out a foot to the far side of the bed and touched Thomasina who mumbled a bit in her sleep. It was good to know someone was there. Jennifer rolled over and finally fell asleep.

3

School Days, School Days

"Oh go away and leave me alone." Jennifer clamped her hands over her ears, so she could hardly hear herself shouting. "Why should I wear these stupid, old-fashioned clothes? Anyhow I don't even want to go to school."

"But Jennifer . . ." Thomasina was looking genuinely puzzled. "We don't have any other kinds of clothes and I gave you my favourite serge dress, the one with the pocket sewn in specially for me. I really am sorry that Josephine threw out your old clothes."

"They were every bit as bad," Jennifer fumed. "I just don't want to wear a skirt or dress to school—period!"

"Then what do you wish to wear?" Benjamin asked.

"JEANS . . ." she started to shout out before realizing that she had already gone too far.

As usual Thom came to the rescue. "It's none of your business what she wears, Benjamin. And you needn't look so superior!"

"Little screaming suffragettes, don't know what they want to wear, don't know what they want . . ."

"If you say that once more you've had it," Jennifer said, clenching her fists.

At that very moment Josephine came rushing into the kitchen with Mother and Father in tow. "Don't say I didn't warn you yesterday about taking in that child. Why the devil himself must be sitting on her tongue. If you ask me she ought to have her mouth washed out with soap."

"Do calm yourself, Josephine." Father cleared his throat as he glanced around the kitchen. "Now what is troubling you three?"

"Nothing," Jennifer sulked.

Benjamin and Thomasina shuffled their feet nervously, while Josephine grabbed a feather duster and began swishing out ashes from the warming oven until she had everyone sneezing.

"Perhaps if we were all to sit down quietly," Mother suggested, giving Josephine an exasperated look. "We have scarcely had time to talk to Jennifer since she arrived and I am sure she must be feeling upset. Benjamin, since you are the eldest, perhaps you can explain exactly what happened this morning."

"Jennifer refused to get ready for school and when we were talking to her she suddenly started yelling and jumping around."

Father looked very stern as his eyebrows came to rest in a steep cliff over his nose. "Hmm, I see. Very well then, Jennifer, if you aren't ready to go to school yet you may help me in my office. I have a patient waiting for me there now who needs to have several boils lanced. And let me see . . . ah yes, there is a suspected case of scarlet fever in town, an infant with whooping cough, a possible measles outbreak nearby . . . "

"Or," Mother suggested, "she could help Josephine and me clean out the cold cellar and air the apple barrels before the new crop arrives. As we very well know, one rotten apple infects the whole barrel." Josephine nodded her head in agreement. "Of course we shall need the lanterns down there in order to swish out the spider webs."

"I never said for sure I wouldn't go to school. It's just that nothing fits me properly and these boots are squinching my toes." Jennifer felt halfway between laughing and crying. Everything was so completely different here. At home she would be pulling on her jeans, slapping together a peanut butter and banana sandwich, yelling "bye Mom, bye Dad,"

as she hurried out the door . . . A knobbly lump was
growing in her throat. She turned away to avoid Father's
questioning look. "Okay, I guess I'll go."

Father and Mother glanced at one another. "I believe
we have more on our hands than we realized," Jennifer
heard him say softly. Then he put his fingers on his lips.
"We must be careful."

"So now that everything is settled," Mother was saying
briskly, "be off to school the three of you before you are
late. And CYK."

"What's that CYK your mother was talking about?"
Jennifer asked Thom as the front door closed behind them.

"Oh nothing, just something our family says."

"It must mean something," Jennifer persisted, "or she
wouldn't have said it."

Thomasina grinned. "You certainly are persistent. All
right then, it means Consider Yourself Kissed. CYK for
short."

"Sounds silly." Jennifer wrinkled her nose.

"I knew you would say that, which is why I didn't want
to tell you in the first place. Why do you think everything
we do or say or wear is so silly? Why, Jennifer? I know
lots of people from the city and they don't think that way.
Promise you will tell me after school where you really
come from."

"What do you mean tell you?" Jennifer asked, alarmed.
"Do you think I've been lying to you or something?"

"Just what I said." Thomasina shrugged her shoulders.

"Aren't you two ever coming!" Benjamin was waiting
a short distance down the road, polishing a russet apple
that he had snitched from an overhanging branch on Mr.
Macklin's tree. He made a mock bow and presented it to
Jennifer. "I picked it for you."

For once Jennifer didn't know what to say.

"You never give me apples," Thom complained.

"That's because you are my sister and anyhow you
spend half your waking hours sitting up in apple trees."

The three of them lapsed into silence as they hurried along the dirt road towards school. Jennifer was relieved to have a few tranquil moments to herself. She needed time to absorb all the differences that kept leaping out at her from every turn in this strangely new, yet old-fashioned world. Having to be constantly on guard, trying to watch each word, was exhausting. It was also lonely. If only she could confide in someone. Perhaps she ought to tell Thom the whole story, at least as far as she understood it herself.

Suddenly a heavily laden wagon drawn by a team of four work horses rumbled past them and Jennifer jumped to the side of the road. Thomasina was watching her closely with that same puzzled expression on her face. "Don't worry, Jennifer. The drivers can usually handle them and if there ever is a runaway all you need to do is stand behind a tree."

"Great!" Jennifer thought, looking all around. "So long as you can find a tree when you need one."

"Does your family have a horse?" Thom asked abruptly.

"Are you crazy! Only millionaires can afford to keep a horse in the city. We have a car like . . . I mean . . . " She had done it again! Thomasina was staring at her all bug-eyed. It was a good thing Benjamin was too far ahead to hear clearly. "I mean more and more people in the city are getting cars . . . er, I should say automobiles." Is that what they called cars way back when? Jennifer hoped so.

Thom gulped. "You mean your family actually owns an automobile like the one rich Mr. Davidson has? His is the only one in town. Nobody likes it because it's so noisy and frightens all the horses along the road."

"Maybe ours isn't quite the same as Mr. Davidson's." Jennifer pictured their own sleek, two-toned model standing beside an old-fashioned car and she couldn't help smiling a bit.

"Say, this is the second time I've had to stop and wait for you two," Benjamin was calling back to them from where he had stopped. "I haven't all morning to waste while you girls dawdle along and gossip."

Thomasina stuck out her tongue at him. "Who said we cared to walk with you, Master Benjamin? Anyhow Jennifer and I are going in here to visit Mr. Purdy to see if he has any spare sweets."

"Then don't blame me when you are late. I'm counting to five and after that I shall leave."

"Good!" Jennifer shouted over her shoulder. "You can count to a thousand for all we care, right Thom?" She caught a quick glimpse of Benjamin's cheeks turning a fiery red before he hurried off.

Thomasina pulled Jennifer after her into the store. "For goodness' sake, Jennifer, if you don't show a speck of smile, Mr. Purdy will never give us a sweet."

"It's that brother of yours. He is so bossy!"

"Oh forget about him," Thomasina sniffed. "Boys are all the same at his age."

"How doth the busy little bees?" a voice at the back of the store called out and Mr. Purdy appeared from behind a row of apple barrels. "You brought a friend of yours along, Thomasina?"

Jennifer felt herself being poked in the back. "Shake hands with him and for goodness' sake, SMILE!" Thom whispered.

Mr. Purdy handed each of them a jelly candy wrapped in bright paper. "Now be off," he smiled, "lest the truant officer catches up with all three of us."

The last ring of the school bell had already died away when Thomasina and Jennifer reached the now empty yard.

"You're the only girl I know who can keep up to me in running," Thomasina panted. "All the others give up so soon. It's downright discouraging."

"Well I'm glad to know there is something good about having long, skinny legs. Mostly I feel clumsy, except when I am running or jumping."

"Sssh," Thom put a warning finger to her mouth. "We

are going to sneak in the back way here so we won't have to go past the principal's office. The door is locked, but I discovered how to open it when I was late three times in a row. Look here.'' After dumping out her school bag, Thom produced a thin piece of metal which she slipped between the crack of the double doors. A few minutes later they were slowly swinging open.

"That was great, Thom. Do you always carry emergency equipment around with you?"

Thomasina nodded. "The best part is that none of the boys know about this secret entrance, not even Archibald, Benjamin's pesky friend. You better follow behind me, Jennifer. With some luck Miss Wishart won't have missed us yet."

The two of them slipped down the hall, past an open classroom where the pupils nearest to the door started sniggering and pointing at the late comers. Luckily the teacher was facing the blackboard and didn't notice anything. Outside the next classroom Jennifer saw a long lineup of children, looking very glum and subdued.

"Whew! We are in luck. Miss Wishart is still at it."

"At what, Thom?"

"Sssh, don't let her catch you talking out loud in the hall. She is a holy terror."

"But what is she doing in there?"

The other children in the lineup turned round to stare at the newcomer who dared to talk out loud.

"Do be careful, Jennifer," Thom whispered again. "Provoking Miss Wishart will only get you into terrible trouble. You see every Monday she has this Deportment class . . . "

"What's that?"

The heads in the lineup all swung round again.

Thomasina tried to go on. "Miss Wishart checks us as we come into her classroom to make sure we are neat and clean, and lectures us about our manners and . . . "

A voice suddenly called out "NEXT" and Thomasina

vanished into the jaws of the classroom. What she had said wasn't exactly encouraging, but before Jennifer had time to work herself into a panic, she too was whisked around the corner, where a very tall, thin woman began inspecting first her hands, then her neck and ears and finally her teeth. "So this is the new child. Ran away from home, so the note to the principal said. What a wicked, wilful thing for a young child to do! What do you have to say for yourself."

"It isn't true."

"What do you mean, child. How dare you talk to me so insolently?"

Thomasina was sitting near the front of the classroom making frantic signs to Jennifer.

"Answer me."

A low ripple ran around the room as Jennifer stood in front of Miss Wishart without saying a word.

"I do not approve of either your manners or your personal appearance, child. Your hair is outrageous, like that of some wild Hottentot and your fingernails are filthy. Let us hope that copying out a list of manners fifty times will teach you how to wear a clean collar over a clean neck and will make you more fastidious in the future. Now go to that empty seat and be silent."

Jennifer felt everyone staring at her as she stumbled towards the desk. "Don't let them see how you are feeling," she told herself, "least of all that old windbag at the front." Why wasn't Thom sitting closer where they could talk or at least see one another? When Jennifer tried to speak to the girl sharing the same double desk, the girl hid her face behind a book.

"Open your books, pupils, and prepare to write. For the time being you may put your practice slates underneath the desks."

Out of the corner of her eye Jennifer watched the girl next to her pick up a pen that looked more like a long pencil and dip it into a hole at the top of her desk. Then she very carefully lifted the pen from the inkwell, tapped it once or twice against the edge to get rid of excess ink and with the same infinite care began to write in her book. Jennifer watched, absolutely fascinated, until she noticed Thom signalling to her from across the room. Oh, oh— Miss Wishart was moving around the class, stopping by the desks to inspect each pupil's progress.

"I better get a move on before she reaches me," Jennifer thought. But it was as if she was frozen at that exact point in time while the world spun on without her. The more she tried to move her pen, the more panicky she felt. Several blobs of ink got spilled across the top of the page.

"Child!" Miss Wishart was suddenly towering over her with a ruler grasped in one fist. The end of the ruler was quivering. "No pupil of mine does such sloppy work." She caught hold of Jennifer's arm. "Spare the rod and spoil the child!" And with that she brought the ruler down on Jennifer's outstretched palm.

Jennifer screamed before the ruler had even touched her hand. "No . . . I'll tell my parents . . . " The scream turned into a cry of pain as the sting from the ruler shot up her arm and mushroomed out into her shoulder until she felt almost sick. Before the ruler could descend for a second time, Jennifer wrenched her arm free. She jumped up from the desk. "You . . . you mean old woman. I hate you. I'll tell the whole world what you are really like." And without another word she ran from the room.

Miss Wishart remained frozen to the spot. There was a moment of silence followed by a low "hummmm," the soft murmur of bees as neighbour whispered to neighbour. By the time Thomasina had jumped up from her seat to see what had become of Jennifer, Miss Wishart had also mobilized herself. She pushed Thom back to her desk.

"SILENCE! I will not countenance such behaviour. Open your grammar books at page 56—Sentence Structure. Thomasina, you will stand up and parse the following sentence, noting especially any subordinate clauses and relative pronouns: Woe betide the child that does not pay strict attention to the words of his elders for he shall reap the whirlwind.''

Jennifer raced blindly down the hallway, almost colliding with the principal as he emerged from his office. "No running!'' he called.

The words echoed through Jennifer's head like a familiar chorus. With eyes half closed she almost expected to find herself back in the museum corridors, the refrain resounding after her, "No run-ning.'' But here she was already sprinting down the steps and out the front door of the school. What a relief to feel the sun and fresh air streaking across her face. Perhaps she would never stop running. What did it matter if the whole town was turning to stare after her. Let them stare! What did it matter if she didn't know where she was going . . .

When Jennifer finally did stop, she found herself standing beside the very straw stack where she had landed— was it eons ago or only yesterday? The quietness of late fall lay over the countryside. A team of workhorses was pulling a plough over the field, but from where Jennifer watched it looked as if a comb was gently touching the last remains of summer. Now and again a bumblebee veered through the stubble, searching out the stray wild aster or clover head which had escaped the cutting. The birds that still remained were silent under the autumn haze, waiting. Jennifer waited too, for what she was not quite sure. Perhaps something would transport her effortlessly back home, where she might catch her parents in the middle of a sentence as though she had only left them in thought for a few seconds.

When nothing happened panic swept over her. "If I can't go back from here, where do I turn next?'' The ghostly line of straw stacks tossed back the question. Then a new fear gripped her. "But what if I can never get back home? Never see my parents, my house, my own room . . . stuck here forever . . .''

Jennifer pulled the twenty-five cent piece from her dress pocket. It felt so small and vulnerable as she cupped it in her hand. Yet it was her only link with that world of Sunday movies and traffic jams which was beginning to feel so remote. She mustn't lose this one too.

Jennifer started slowly back towards town. There was no point in standing around an empty field. She might just as well return to the house. If she was lucky the grownups would be out and she could escape their endless questions, at least for a while. What had been an adventure at first was now turning into a nightmare. How was she going to find a way to escape? Somehow Jennifer's thoughts kept returning to Thom, that weird kid with the gangling legs, the pointed nose and the funny way of talking. Didn't sound exactly promising . . . and yet, Jennifer thought, I feel so close to her, like a sister almost. Perhaps she could believe my story. Perhaps we could be real friends. And maybe, somehow, they could find an answer together. Jennifer sighed. "Real friends—it isn't so easy completely trusting another person."

From the road Jennifer spotted the row of lilacs leading up to the old brick house. She turned into the lane, opened the gate in the picket fence and crept around the side of the house. From far off in the garden she could hear Josephine singing a patriotic marching song. Neither Mother nor Father appeared to be at home yet. Good! Jennifer stole into the kitchen, grabbed two of Josephine's cinnamon muffins from the pantry shelf and ate them both on the spot. Afterwards she tiptoed upstairs. As she was about to flop down on Thomasina's bed she noticed a ladder standing near the door to the room. The longer Jennifer stared at the ladder, the more curious she grew.

"What a chance!" Jennifer thought. There was still no sound from downstairs. Quickly she scrambled up the ladder and pushed on the trap door in the ceiling until it tilted back. A shower of dust and cobwebs rained down on her head. It looked as if no one had been there for ages. "Hold your sneeze,'' Jennifer told herself sternly, as she wriggled up through the hole.

Without bothering to look around the attic Jennifer replaced the trap door. ''Whew, that's better!'' Now if anyone did come upstairs they wouldn't see that gaping hole, nor would they suspect she was in the attic. What a super hiding place it made! Jennifer sat quietly for a moment until her breathing calmed down and her eyes became accustomed to the dim light. It was difficult not to feel like an intruder, surrounded as she was by other people's castoffs and half forgotten treasures.

On one side of the room was a small window, through which the early afternoon sun was slanting a few warm rays. A crisscross pattern of light moved back and forth on the ceiling as a tree branch scratched against the glass. Except for Jennifer's breathing it was the only sound. Rows of boxes lined the wall, clothes covered with sheets hung from huge wooden pegs, toys lay neglected on the floor, along with dust-covered books and shoes that didn't match. But more interesting to Jennifer was a black and white rocking horse standing under the window. When she was a little kid she had always wanted a rocking horse exactly like that one—a genuine rocking horse, the kind of magical one you read about in stories. Jennifer took a step towards it.

Thump! The horse began to sway on its rockers; into the shadows and back through the light, into the shadows and back . . . Jennifer watched half-hypnotised, her mind running over all the stories she had ever read about haunted attics and ghostly children returning to claim their long lost toys. Another thump, almost a crash. The rocking horse was going crazy.

Jennifer began to giggle. A family of squirrels was using the rocking horse as a springboard to leap onto the window sill where they were escaping under the frame which was slightly ajar. Jennifer covered her mouth to stiffle her half hysterical giggles. Already the squirrels were halfway to the ground, spinning and leaping down a thickly braided rope attached to a hook just inside the window. "That looks like a fun way of going down," Jennifer thought. "Now if I can push this window up a bit." It wouldn't budge.

As she was looking around for a broom handle or stick with which to lever the window, she heard a voice calling from nearby. "Jennifer, Jennifer."

"Damn those noisy squirrels anyhow!" Someone must have heard all the racket from the attic. But how did they find out she was there? Jennifer crouched down behind an old barrel.

"There is no use hiding, Jennifer. I know precisely where you are."

Whose voice was that and where was it coming from? There was a slight creak, the trap door moved up and a hand reached through.

"Thom . . . Benjamin?" Jennifer asked weakly.

But there was no reply as an old-fashioned camera rose through the opening, followed by the dark figure of a man.

"The . . . the photographer from the museum!" Even the words froze inside Jennifer's mouth. Like a trapped animal she felt herself turning prickly all over, then numb.

"Fancy finding you here, child—how fortunate! Not that I can actually see you yet, but time will take care of that, as time takes care of everything."

The mocking voice crept into every corner of the attic. Jennifer felt the shadow of it rolling towards her hiding place, like some monster with searching tentacles. "Ah, there you are in your hiding place, my dear child. How very clever of you to come up here all alone, away from the hustle and bustle of people. I too enjoy the peacefulness of this place; old clothes, discarded toys, dusty photographs . . . Oh how I detest the modern, garish things one sees nowadays. Yes, you are a clever child in spite of your wicked tongue. Boring was how you described my collection of photographs, I believe? You do invite trouble, my child. I chose you knowing full well your wilful ways would lead you on and on . . . So now you shall be staying here among my seen and not heard children . . . one year . . . ten years, it matters not. Are you shaking your head?''

"I can't stay," Jennifer managed to break in at last. "I won't. My dad told me to be back in half an hour. You can't make me stay."

"Come, come, child. If you learn nothing else you will come to know that time, as you so foolishly speak of it, means nothing to me. Forever is but a fleeting second. I brought you here, so now only I can transport you back to that other time of yours."

Jennifer felt the weight of those words dragging her down, down, in an endless spiral. Her head was spinning; she could scarcely see.

"Jennifer!" Thomasina was calling from outside, but the sound broke into the darkness of the attic. "It's me— Thom. I've been looking all over for you, ever since we got out from school. If you're anywhere around the house, please answer me . . . There is nothing to worry about, I've already talked to Father."

"Pay no attention to that detestable child out there; all helter-skelter, forever chattering . . . And now I shall draw my camera closer for another photograph of the 'seen and not heard child.' Surely you remember the first one which I took inside the museum? How forgetful the child grows already!''

"No, I won't . . . I won't be one of your 'seen and not heard children.' You're lying! I came here by myself. My 'willful ways' brought me here—those were your very words. I don't belong here."

"I'm afraid you have no choice now, Jennifer," the voice went on.

"But I do, I must . . . I'm coming Thom . . . Wait for me, wherever you are." Jennifer wrenched one of the loose barrel staves free and rammed it with such force under the window that the frame split open. The glass shattered on the floor. At the same instant there was an explosive flash from the camera.

"Jennifer—How on earth did you get there!" Thomasina looked up from the ground to see a pair of legs kicking through the attic window and the rope twisting about like a crazy serpent. "Careful, Jennifer. Don't jerk too hard. That rope has been there for ages. Father put it there in case of fire. I think it would be safer to swing onto the kitchen roof and come the rest of the way by ladder. Good!" Thomasina breathed a huge sigh of relief when Jennifer managed to get a foothold on the roof. "And hurry! Josephine is right under your feet now and she has a habit of hearing herds of elephants everywhere."

Jennifer half jumped, half fell from the ladder into Thom's outstretched arms.

"Oof, you weren't supposed to completely flatten me! I was just standing here to give you confidence." Thom managed a crushed sort of grin as she grabbed the end of the rope to toss it back on the kitchen roof. But instead the rope came flying down to the ground. Her face turned pale on inspecting the break. "You see here Jennifer? The top was cut off with a knife or something else sharp. There is no sign of its fraying or coming loose with your weight." Thomasina looked straight at Jennifer. "As I said earlier, I think you have some explaining to do."

Jennifer nodded her head weakly. "You're right, Thom and I just hope you aren't furious with me for all the fuss with Miss Wishart and . . . and everything else." She could barely finish the sentence because she felt so sick to her stomach.

"Jennifer—you look awful. Wait a minute, I'll run and fetch some water from the pump. Then when you are feeling a little better we can climb up to my fort in the Duchess apple tree where no one can pester us."

The fort was lodged between two gnarled limbs of the apple tree, with planks making up the floor, and a tangle of branches plus a few boards forming the sides and roof.

"It's really super, Thom."

"Thanks. I made it all by myself. Benjamin is a tiny bit jealous if I do say so."

"Say, where is your brother? Is he liable to come prowling around and bothering us?"

"I doubt it. He went tearing off somewhere, looking for you." She looked at Jennifer slyly. "He looked terribly concerned when he heard you had run away, which is unusual because he dislikes girls as a matter of principle."

"And I dislike boys," Jennifer added quickly, to chase away any notions that might have been lurking in Thom's mind, "at least until they are as old as grandfathers." The girls laughed.

For a few moments they were silent, each waiting for the other one to speak. Finally Jennifer began, knowing that it was up to her to tell Thom what had happened. Listening to herself talk, it all sounded so unreal, like someone else's voice retelling a story or movie they had once seen together a long time ago. Every so often Thomasina would whistle through her teeth, completely ignoring Josephine's oft-repeated warning about whistling girls and crowing hens coming to some bad end. Afterwards she just stared at Jennifer as though she were a ghost or a visitor from another planet. She reached over to pinch Jennifer's arm.

"Hey, ouch! I do feel that, Thom."

The spell was broken. They weren't strangers staring at each other across some empty space, but two friends laughing together.

"It's our secret, Jennifer. For the time being we won't tell another soul, agreed?"

Jennifer nodded. "Think of the fun we can have together, Thom, feeling sort of superior because nobody else knows our secret . . . If only it weren't for that photographer . . . What if he is telling the truth . . ."

"You mustn't listen to him Jennifer. And don't let him take another picture of you, either. I have a strange feeling he may be trying to gain power over you or means to harm you in some way. Let's hope we never see him again."

They both shivered. "I'm going to call him Mr. Blackwood," Jennifer said at last, "because a name makes him seem less terrible."

"Talking of terrible things," Thomasina said, trying to change the subject, "I think I heard my brother."

A few minutes later Benjamin appeared around the corner of the house, his face completely red from running. "Thomasina, where are you?"

"Up here in my tree house. But you can't come up now."

"So aren't you a fine one, sitting up there like a bird while I'm running all over the countryside looking for her! She isn't anywhere, Thom. I even looked by the straw stacks where we first found her."

Thomasina motioned to Jennifer to stay quiet. "What do you care about her anyways, Benjamin?"

"Well, you can't let people disappear without doing anything, can you?"

"Even if it's a no-good girl?"

"I never said . . . say why aren't you looking for her?" Benjamin asked suspiciously when he heard a giggle from the tree.

"Because Jennifer is up here with me and has been for the last half hour."

"You two! I ought to tell Mother and Father all about the trouble at school."

"It won't do you any good, Mr. Tattle-tale, because I have already spoken to Father. You know he has no use for teachers who beat their pupils. He has seen too many hurt children and Miss Wishart knows that too."

"I was never going to tell anyhow," Benjamin grumbled. He sat down under the tree. "Are you two ever coming down?"

"In a minute," Jennifer replied sweetly. "Meanwhile, here is something to keep you busy." She dropped a left-over apple on Benjamin's head.

A few seconds later it flew back up. "It's all wormy. Eat it yourself," and Benjamin stomped off into the house.

Thomasina and Jennifer stayed up in the tree house talking until the lengthening shadows across the garden told them it was almost supper time.

4

Ring out Wild Bells

"I'd be ever so glad if you would stop licking your fingers, Thomasina. The sound is disgusting and it's also very unsanitary." Benjamin plunked down his school bag in front of the kitchen stove and kicked off his boots.

"Says who!" Jennifer scarcely looked up from the pot of maple cream which she was stirring over the stove. "People who have to stay in late after school shouldn't complain."

"It wasn't my fault! Mr. Skinner always keeps his class in on Hallowe'en just to be mean."

"Ha, some excuse!"

"Woeful waste makes woeful want," Thomasina remarked piously, licking the last bit of pull taffy off her fingers and staring at her brother.

"I beg your pardon, Thomasina?" Josephine had just come into the kitchen, her arms laden down with jars of fruit preserves from the cold cellar. There was a hint of a smile on her face. "Did I hear something about waste? And why is that perfectly fine piece of bacon still sitting on your supper plate?"

"It's all fat," Thomasina complained, returning to the table. "See?" She impaled the morsel of bacon on the end of her fork.

Josephine stood over her watching the last swallow going down. "There now, that's better."

Benjamin stifled a laugh as he hurried from the kitchen. "Don't forget the party at Archibald's house tonight—

seven o'clock sharp. And don't go and wear your tattiest old clothes, Thomasina. You need either a fancy costume or your Sunday best.'' He looked as though he was about to say something to Jennifer, but deciding against it pulled out his pocket watch. "It is now exactly five o'clock. Remember we don't want to be late; in precisely one hour and a half we ought to be leaving.''

"Yes, brother dear," Thomasina muttered under her breath.

Jennifer left the maple cream to cool beside the window and came over to the kitchen table. "Honestly, Thom, if I were you I wouldn't put up with his bossy behaviour. Why don't you stand up to him, tell him to go jump in the lake or something?''

"I do, Jennifer, but it gets so tiresome. And you know everyone encourages him—you're the eldest Benjamin, now you are responsible . . . ''

They were quiet together for a few minutes until Josephine came flouncing back into the kitchen. "I thought I told you to soak the pots in water immediately, before they became all crusted over with toffee," she fumed. "Hallowe'en . . . hmmph . . . an excuse for gluttony and foolish pranks if you ask me.''

Jennifer poked her friend. "We better vanish upstairs.''

After a few minutes of checking through her wardrobe Thomasina announced, "I don't feel like wearing my last year's costume and the sight of my good dresses makes me sick.''

"I agree.''

"What shall we wear then? We don't have that much time and we still have to pack the maple cream to take to Archibald's.''

"Wait a minute Thom . . . I have this really great idea. Why don't we dress the way I used to back home? For sure you'll feel comfy.''

"So what do we need?''

"First of all pants . . . um . . . trousers, like your father

48

wears, I guess; then let's see, maybe a blouse or sweater, I mean cardigan. If we can get hold of a couple of Benjamin's crazy caps that would be great and of course running shoes, but since you don't have any, maybe we can wear work boots and pretend we are going hiking . . . ''

As Jennifer paused for breath a wave of homesickness surged over her. If only she could step inside her own home for one moment, yell out "Hi, Mom, Hi, Dad," run up the stairs to her room, bang the door shut, wiggle her toes in the cosy rug beside the bed, turn on her radio full blast . . .

"Look at what I've got already." Thomasina was bent over a cedar chest out in the hall. Two caps were sitting on her head and several pairs of her father's old trousers were draped over her shoulder.

"Do you think they'll mind us ransacking the old clothes chest, Thom?"

"I hope not, because it's too late to worry now," Thom mumbled through a blouse hanging from her mouth. "We shall have to look for boots in the woodshed."

A few minutes later they were admiring themselves in Mother's bedroom mirror. "My hair," Thom was fuming, "my hair doesn't look proper under this cap. Let's cut it Jennifer, right now, before I have time to change my mind."

"But Thom, what will your parents say and there's Josephine to worry about as well . . . I can practically see the expression on her face."

Thomasina pulled a pair of shears from her mother's sewing basket. "Here! Now cut it—please. Aren't you the one who is always telling me to stand up to people, not care what they say? And now you are turning into a regular jellyroll yourself."

That was enough for Jennifer. With shaking hands she grabbed the shears, stuffed a wad of Thom's hair between the blades and forced the handles together. They wouldn't shut properly; there was too much hair wedged in there. Jennifer yanked some strands out.

"Ouch! I said cut my hair, not pull it out by the roots."

"Sorry, Thom. I'm a bit nervous."

Snip! The right side of Thomasina's hair drifted to the floor. Snip, snip, snip! Now the back fell off. Jennifer surveyed her work with dismay. It was all crooked. What were they always saying in the olden days—a woman's crowning glory was her hair—or something like that? So maybe she had done a terrible thing to her friend. Maybe it was like robbing a church. Snip, snip, snip! The left and final side floated reproachfully to the floor. Jennifer scuffed the hair under Mother's chaise lounge so Thom couldn't see how much had gone. She gave her the hand mirror.

"You can look now. It . . . it's not quite even everywhere and as I said I'm no expert hair cutter . . . I mean you wanted it cut didn't you Thom?" Suddenly Jennifer burst into tears. "Oh, Thom, I've gone and wrecked it for you. It will take ages to grow back and by that time you will be all hunched over and white haired."

Thomasina was staring straight into the mirror which was trembling ever so slightly in her hand. A single tear appeared in the corner of one eye, but she brushed it away. "It's marvelous, just what I always wanted, but never dared do anything about until you came along." She hugged Jennifer. "No more rags tied around my hair at night to make curls, no more terrible tangles, no more braids!" She pulled the cap right down over her head.

The two of them stood side by side, arm and arm, staring into the mirror. Jennifer was smiling now. "You could be my twin almost. I wish you could come back and live with me, Thom."

"And I wish you could stay here forever and ever."

"Forever and ever"—the words were like the tolling of a bell falling between them, creating a black chasm that no arms could bridge. And from out of the darkness rose an even darker figure, that of the old photographer, Mr. Blackwood, blotting out their images in the mirror. But when he swirled his cloak towards them it fell away harmless, because it could not encircle the two of them together.

"Thom?"

"Uh huh . . . "

"I was just wondering how you were . . . "

"Thomasina! Jennifer! Where are you two anyhow?" Benjamin was calling from the landing. "We ought to be leaving in ten minutes." When he looked up from consulting his watch, Thomasina was staring him in the face. "My cap—you're wearing my cap. And you hair, great galloping ghosts, what have you done to your hair, Thomasina?"

"Cut it all off. Good riddance to bad rubbish."

"Just wait until everyone sees you!"

"Who cares! I'm going to run like a gazelle now and swim and dive like a whale. And when I come out of the water I shall shake my head in the sunlight and the drops will fly and sparkle everywhere and my hair will be dry and beautiful as a butterfly's wings in two seconds. So there!"

"Just wait till Mother sees you. What are you two supposed to be anyhow, a couple of tramps?"

"We're wearing sensible things, the way girls will in the future," Jennifer retorted.

"With hair and clothes like that nobody could tell the girls from the boys."

"Oh there would be ways of telling still." Jennifer gave Benjamin a wicked look.

He blushed and stared at his feet. "Anyhow, I shall be down in the kitchen. I can't wait to see the expression on Josephine's face."

When they came downstairs a few minutes later Josephine took one horrified look and rushed from the kitchen. "I swear on the Holy Bible I had nothing to do with it," they heard her saying out in the hall.

Mother appeared at the kitchen door. "Your hair Thomasina—you cut your beautiful hair. How could you do such a thing!"

"It wouldn't fit under my cap properly, so I had to cut it all off."

Mother looked at the two of them without saying anything. Finally, "Well, what's done cannot be undone. It will grow back in time, I expect."

Father had just closed his office door on the last patient of the day. When he saw the two girls standing in front of him he barely flicked an eyebrow. "So the twins are ready for the party tonight, are they? You did a remarkable job, Jennifer."

What does he mean by that remark anyhow, Jennifer wondered to herself.

"Let me see now," Father continued, "what are you two supposed to be? How about 'Ladies League of the New Twentieth Century' . . . What do you say to that title, Jennifer?"

She pretended to laugh, but muttered to Thom on the side, "It makes me nervous when he keeps talking to me. I get this feeling he knows all about me . . . "

"We are already five minutes late in leaving," Benjamin reminded them.

"Then be off with you bold, brave ladies," Father said, giving them a good natured push towards the front door.

Mother added a few, last minute words of warning. "Now remember to thank Archibald's parents after the party. And most important of all—don't stay out after curfew. If you hear the warning bell from the town hall run home quickly so Paddy Maines won't have a chance to catch you. Don't forget Benjamin, as the eldest you are in charge . . . " Mother waved to the three of them from the open door. "CYK."

"Who is this Paddy Maines anyhow?" Jennifer asked.

"Count yourself lucky for not having met him yet," Thomasina replied, making a face. "He's our town constable and his favourite occupation is reporting children who have broken the curfew, even if they are only a tiny speck late . . . "

"Like you always are, Thomasina," Benjamin couldn't resist adding.

"Well, he's never been able to catch me, so there!"

The front door had barely closed when Jennifer remembered she had left her cap sitting on the kitchen table.

"And hurry!" Benjamin called back to her.

As Jennifer slipped down the hallway she could hear Mother and Father talking. "Maude, we really must come to some decision regarding Jennifer's future. The child insists her family is living in Toronto and yet we have been unable to find out anything. We've contacted orphanages, placed notices in the dailies . . . all to no avail. And now this letter arrives from some city official . . ."

Jennifer could hear the rustle of paper as she listened outside the parlour room door.

"Dear Sir, In reply to your recent request for information about a certain Jennifer Martz, we can locate no family with that surname presently residing in Toronto . . ."

Jennifer felt a shiver running across her shoulders at the sound of those words, "no family with that surname . . ." She was indeed lost.

"It appears to me, Timothy, that we have no choice at the present," Mother was saying. "Whether the child is telling us the complete truth or not, she really must stay with us. Think of the alternatives—an orphanage perhaps? You know too well what that would be like. Besides Thomasina would never hear of us sending her new-found friend back to Toronto. You saw what a raggle-taggle pair they made this evening.?"

Jennifer heard Father chuckling. "Yes indeed . . . But there is something troubling me, Maude. I felt it more strongly than ever this evening. If I weren't a scientific man I might almost think . . ." He hesitated and tapped his fingers on the table.

"Yes, I know. I too have felt it, almost an alien quality about the child . . ."

"Say, are you ever coming?" Benjamin called through the front door. "It's getting later and later and we shall be missing the best part of the evening."

Jennifer ducked away from the parlour and out the front door before the grownups had seen her. After leaving the house the darkness completely enveloped the three of them. Jennifer looked back once or twice before they turned onto the main road, but there was only a tiny pinprick of light showing from the house, like a ship floating alone on a vast sea.

"It won't be so dark nearer town," Thom reassured her.

As they walked along Jennifer tried to describe how it looked at night where she lived. Thomasina listened in quiet disbelief until she could no longer contain herself. "You mean a thousand times brighter than at my grandparents' place in the city? You really mean that . . . "

"Way more! Imagine a huge firework display going on all around you, cars and flashing signs everywhere and high above you the lights of skyscrapers and maybe a jet plane shooting off into space . . . "

"Skyscraper . . . jet . . . ?"

Faced with a new batch of explanations, it was Jennifer's turn to throw up her hands helplessly.

The only sound now was the steady scrunch, scrunch of their feet along the gravel road. Benjamin was walking ahead of the two others, holding the small candle lantern that Father had given him. Jennifer opened and closed her eyes several times. Except for the bobbing speck of candlelight it didn't make much difference. You could eat carrots until you burst, she decided, but it still wouldn't help you to see any better in this blackness. Black as the inside out of a dream! Her thoughts kept travelling back to that terrible, shut-off room in the museum . . .

When Thom spoke up a few minutes later her voice sounded strained. Jennifer jumped and Benjamin must have too, because the candlelight suddenly swerved to one side. "Jennifer . . . do you remember that story about the headless horseman and how he chases Ichabod Crane one dark night and throws his head after him?"

"When they are galloping over the bridge," Jennifer

added. At any other time it would have been super fun sharing a story they both knew so well, but now . . .

"Thomasina, couldn't you tell that story some other time?" Benjamin's voice was strained.

"I couldn't help thinking about it because the bridge over Brewer's Creek is just ahead. And if there is anything or anybody lurking around it's better to be talking to show we aren't scared."

The scrunch of gravel underfoot suddenly gave way to a hollow thud, thud, thud—they were over the bridge. At that same instant Thomasina burst into song:

Jesus loves me this I know
For the Bible tells me so . . .

Benjamin dropped the lantern he was so startled and the candle was snuffed out. "For heaven's sake Thomasina, now look what you have gone and done with your scatter-brained behaviour. Couldn't you have given us some warning?"

"Never mind," Jennifer interrupted. "I can see the first house up ahead and there seems to be a fire or something burning by the side of the road." As they drew closer Jennifer saw what looked like three demon figures leaping through the smoke billowing up from a pile of burning leaves.

"Walk past as if you don't notice them," Benjamin warned the other two, "and if we are lucky they may leave us alone. Those boys are as tough as nails. I've heard tell their father beats them every night because he always suspects they have been into some trouble or other."

However, the boys had already spotted them. "Well now, look who's happening along; the goody-good children off to a party, I warrant, and the new girl too. Let's make her jump over the fire."

"Oh no you won't!" Benjamin dropped the candle lantern and threw off his jacket. "The first fellow who touches her will feel my fist in his face."

The biggest of the three lunged at Benjamin, but in the

flickering light slipped on some leaves and fell sprawling at Jennifer's feet. She prodded him with her boot. "Shut your stupid mouth, punk. I can jump your puny fire any old day." And with that Jennifer leaped over the flames in one easy motion.

For a moment, the toughies were too stunned to move. Benjamin was very casually pulling on his jacket. "Don't say a word or even look back," he whispered to Jennifer. "Just walk straight ahead—it's not far now to Archibald's house."

"Bravo, Jennifer!" Thom patted her on the back.

Jennifer could feel her legs shaking, the same feeling she had once had when a dog trailed after her for a whole block growling and sniffing at her ankles before finally losing interest. Where was that house anyhow! The toughies were screaming at them, but they didn't seem to be following. Finally Benjamin pulled her through a gate and up to a house where two jack o'lanterns were smiling at them through the window. "Whew, what a relief!"

"You sounded positively ferocious with those bullies," Benjamin remarked, gradually loosening his grip on Jennifer's arm.

"Even if my knees were shaking like the leaves on a popular tree!" Jennifer grinned back. "And you weren't so bad yourself."

Thomasina lifted the knocker on the door and let it fall with a thud. The door opened with a terrible roar. A bear was standing on its back legs in the open doorway, waving a pair of massive paws at them. Seeing how startled the three of them looked, the bear removed its head, which turned out to be a fur hat, and Archibald's father emerged from a buffalo skin coat to welcome them into a houseful of laughing children.

Jennifer found herself being propelled down a long hallway towards a room where even more children were sitting cross-legged in a semicircle. In the centre a tiny girl with monstrous spectacles balanced on her nose had just started reciting:

Children, you are very little
And your bones are very brittle
If you would grow great and stately
You must try to walk sedately . . .

"Oh no!" Jennifer groaned out loud.

"Sssh," Benjamin hissed in her ear. "You want to disgrace us all in front of Archibald's family and guests?"

Jennifer looked around desperately for Thom who had somehow gotten separated from them. It was a relief to see her on the other side of the room, winking and making a crazy face back at them. "What a dumb way to spend Hallowe'en," Jennifer complained, "cooped up in a room listening to some blubbery little kid."

Benjamin leaned over, "So what would you rather be doing this evening?"

Without thinking she blurted out, "I'd like to be out trick or treating, that's what, collecting piles of candy n' stuff, prowling around with the other kids in the dark and having FUN. And then I'd sort out all my junk at home on the living room rug. Dad would have a fire going for me too, I bet," she added half to herself.

Jennifer hadn't exactly been whispering and when people started nudging each other and turning around to stare, Benjamin's face turned scarlet. But the tiny, spectacled reciter was pressing on to her triumphant conclusion:

But the unkind and the unruly
And the sort who eat unduly
They must never hope for glory
Theirs is quite a different story!

As it came to an end, Thomasina slithered across the floor towards her brother, mumbling something unintelligible through a mouthful of divinity fudge.

"Thomasina, polite people do not talk and eat at the same time."

"Stop being so beastly, Benjamin. You sound exactly like Josephine."

"Who is the beastly one I'd like to know? I'm supposed

to keep us out of trouble, but ever since *she* arrived there has been nothing but trouble.''

"Perhaps we ought to ask Father to send her away then?''

Benjamin looked sour and stalked away to join Archibald and some of his other friends who were bobbing for apples.

"I'm sorry Thom, you know Benjamin is right. Everywhere I go I get into trouble.''

"Just like me." Thom squeezed her hand. "Come on. Let's show those boys how to bob for apples.''

Thomasina had finally managed to soak Archibald's head with water from the huge tub and he was splashing water back, when bells started ringing. A hush fell over the party as the sound broke into the house, filling everyone's ears, until the whole room exploded with one word: "FIRE!''

They rushed to the front door. A glow was spreading across the sky on the other side of town. Every so often a flame shot upwards like a sun gone crazy. And with the rising wind the panic call of the bells came in endless waves. Fire, fire, fire . . . Jennifer felt her heart thumping wildly, urging her feet towards that terrifying, yet fascinating light.

An adult's voice cut through the spreading panic in the hallway. "The help of every grown person is needed at the fire. And as for you children, it is almost nine o'clock and time to be going home.''

Benjamin was eyeing his pocket watch and moving towards the front door, but suddenly Thom blocked his way. "Can't you take a little risk? Do you always have to be so responsible? Self control, self discipline . . . every day of the year it's the same old thing. No wonder Jennifer thinks we are boring! And do you know what? I think perhaps she is right. Can't you hear those bells calling to us?''

Benjamin hesitated. "You don't need to be so warlike, Thomasina. I'm not deaf. I suppose we could go, but not for very long. We shall have to keep a smart lookout for

Paddy Maines. I'm not sure it's a sensible idea . . . '' And then the three of them were running, dodging and twisting like half-crazed moths towards the fire.

"Fellow put damp hay in his barn. That's how it started," a voice called along the road. "Let's hope it won't spread to the house."

The sound of galloping hooves and warning cries overtook them a few minutes later. There was barely time to leap to the side of the road before a fire wagon pulled by three immense horses roared past. Around one more corner and the heat from the flames brought them to a standstill. Jennifer had to cover her face. It was completely hopeless. The firewagon was so puny and the figures in the human chain passing buckets of water back and forth to douse the flames looked like a bunch of ants. Jennifer thought of the huge fire engines that sometimes wailed past her own house in the middle of the night.

"Aaaah . . . '' a cry rose from the crowd and all faces turned upwards as the barn roof shrivelled and collapsed into the flames.

"Concentrate on the house . . . the barn's gone," one of the firemen yelled.

Sparks from the falling roof were beginning to settle on the shingles, already dried out by the late fall sun. The old man who owned the house was hunched up in a rocking chair, moaning to himself as he rocked back and forth. A dark figure, occasionally illuminated by the flames, was standing beside him, peering intently around at the crowd.

"If you ask me that's Paddy Maines," Benjamin whispered. "You see, I warned you we would get into trouble if we came here."

"Has he noticed us yet?" Jennifer asked.

Thom pointed silently at the dark figure which was now edging its way around the crowd towards them. Paddy Maines had seen them all right. The firelight shone on his face and reflected off something he was carrying in one hand. The three of them stared for a moment as if hypnotised and then the next instant they were running away.

Jennifer looked back over her shoulder once. Was it really Paddy Maines as Benjamin had said? Or was it perhaps Mr. Blackwood, pursuing her alone and crying out above the pounding of their footsteps, "You're too late. Sometime I'll catch you unawares, because I have time, time . . . "

Thomasina, who was ahead of the other two, suddenly swerved to the right and disappeared. They could hear her calling, "I discovered this secret alleyway once behind Mr. Purdy's store. Hurry!"

"Good for you, Thom," Benjamin gasped. "Let's hope we have lost him."

"If only it was a bit darker," Thom complained.

The moon had come up and was dodging in and out of storm-tossed clouds. A figure appeared at the entrance to the alleyway, clearly outlined by the moonlight, then vanished. So he knew where they were hiding!

"Did you see what he was carrying? It must have been a knife or gun—something metallic anyhow. I could see it shining in the moonlight," Jennifer insisted.

"Paddy Maines always carries a truncheon," Benjamin explained. "He doesn't need any weapons like a knife or gun."

"But if it isn't him," Jennifer muttered under her breath.

Thom stared at her in silent understanding. "Well, we don't have time to worry about that now. I know another way out of here with enough twists and turns to fool anybody. Come on!"

No one said a word. Jennifer could feel the wild pounding of her heart bursting into her head and all over her body. The hunter and the hunted—now she knew how a deer feels when every muscle is tuned to the escape.

"I think we have slipped through his fingers," Thomasina said at last. "We've doubled-back on our tracks twice now."

"Can't be too sure," Benjamin replied. "Remember last time! Better keep on running till we reach home—that is if you can."

"Huh!" Thomasina shook her head like a horse's mane. "I could keep going forever. How about you, Jennifer?"

"Same here."

After a while they felt the cool softness of snowflakes sliding across their faces. They were floating effortlessly through space covering incredible distances, their feet no longer jarring their bodies with each step. Forever and ever, Jennifer remembered thinking. No hunter could stop then now.

The next thing Jennifer heard was Thom yawning and saying, "I'm so tired it's even an effort getting into bed."

"How did I get into this crazy nightgown so quickly?" Jennifer wondered aloud. But the lump on the other side of the bed was already sleeping and couldn't hear a thing. After checking to make sure that her precious twenty-five cent piece was safely stowed under the pillow, soon she too was sound asleep.

5

Miles to Go Before I Sleep

Jennifer stretched an icy foot over to Thomasina's side of the bed. There was nobody there. Jennifer jerked her foot back and coiled herself into a shivering ball in the middle of the bed where the quilt seemed lumpiest. Although a thin wisp of smoke was escaping from the stovepipe that ran past the bed and into the roof, there did not seem to be the least bit of heat in it. Jennifer grumbled to herself while she rubbed the two icy blocks that were her feet. Getting up too quickly in the morning always made her feel cross. Anyhow it was Saturday, so why the big rush to spring out of bed? As usual Josephine was clanking around the kitchen, banging pot lids, slamming the oven door, dropping firewood; probably on purpose too in case anyone is still sleeping, Jennifer thought to herself. "Well, you won't get me up. I'm planning to lie here, peacefully thinking."

A peaceful moment—there wasn't much chance of that! If Josephine wasn't nagging about something, Thomasina would be telling her some crazy story or joke. And always Benjamin was hovering in the background, not saying much, but forever wanting to give her things—an apple, a prize chunk of quartz, a treasured stamp . . . A frown crossed Jennifer's face. Even though he bothered her, sometimes . . . secretly . . . she didn't really mind him. Jennifer shook the thought of him away.

And then there was home—the home that she scarcely had time to think about in the beginning as she was tossed from one new experience to the next. Now little things kept reminding her of it; an odd word here or there, a twinkle in Father's eye, a smile from Mother, and suddenly she would find herself staring into space, forgetting where she was or what she had been saying. Funny, but it was the little things she missed the most; talking to her mom after school, telling Dad how she had made the new basketball team . . . How to get back! Jennifer kept pushing the thought away because it seemed to be so hopelessly bound up with the dark figure of Mr. Blackwood. Besides, she didn't have a clue where she should start. "I mean, how am I supposed to know how to get home when I'm not even sure how I got here in the first place!"

Jennifer stopped. Had she been talking out loud, was that shrill sounding voice her own? She rolled herself into a tighter ball underneath the quilt. How to get home . . . how to get home . . . The question kept nagging at her. Mr. Blackwood knows, Mr. Blackwood knows, the clock on the chest of drawers seemed to answer back.

From downstairs, Thomasina's voice came filtering through the stovepipe, like an orchestra being tuned up. "I don't see why I have to wear my winter clothes quite yet. I hate these scratchy, old stockings. They're enough to spoil winter for me."

Josephine's voice, sounding very cross answered her, followed by the kitchen door banging shut. Thom's final, "I don't care a pin!" collided with Mother's voice.

"That is quite enough for one day, Thomasina. Every winter we have this same old fuss about clothes. You will go to your room and stay there. Josephine and I are going shopping and your father is working in his office. Perhaps by this afternoon you will be in a better frame of mind."

Jennifer could hear Thomasina's footsteps stomping along the hallway and starting up the stairs. "If Thom's coming I might as well get up," she decided.

Jennifer aimed her feet into Thom's conveniently waiting slippers and flopped over to the window. Sprong! When she touched the blind it shot into an impossible-to-reach roll at the very top of the window frame. It always did that when she was upset. Jennifer had to shield her eyes. The sun was unbelievably bright, reflecting off a fall of snow that had touched everything—roofs, distant church spire, stubble fields and the forest that slipped over the hills and far away. Even the robin's nest that clung to the window ledge held an oval of white in its centre.

Thomasina burst into the room.

"You finally got up, did you? I brought you something in case you are hungry." Thom opened her hand to reveal a squashed chunk of bread, covered with plum jam.

"You've left half the jam on your fingers," Jennifer complained, taking the bread without even thanking her friend.

Thom slurped the jam off each finger, very slowly and deliberately. "Benjamin hates it when I do this."

"I can see why," Jennifer mumbled.

"Seeing as I have to stay in all morning I might as well enjoy being horrid, disgusting, vile, whatever Josephine would call it. Don't you agree?"

"I don't know what you're jabbering on about!"

"It means I'm cross, irritable, exactly rotten feeling," Thomasina burst out. "Just like you are right now. Only you seem to think I should always look pleased and long-suffering in spite of what you say or do. But I'm not. And what's more I wager if you hadn't been so grumpy and miserable in the first place, Mr. Blackwood would never have been able to lure you here and . . . and . . . " Suddenly Thom burst out crying. "I didn't mean it Jennifer. I didn't. Oh I am sorry . . . truly."

On principle Jennifer didn't believe in crying. If a kid at school cried it was usually because she was acting girlish and blubbery. But with Thom it was very different . . . the tears were coming from far down. Jennifer put an arm around her shoulder. "I'm really sorry, too. I don't want to be mean or fight. You're the best friend I've ever had."

Thom sniffed once or twice and managed a crooked smile. "The same with me."

Jennifer went on. "It's just that I have been feeling so strange recently, as if I don't belong anywhere, anymore. I feel I ought to be trying to get home, but I don't know where to start, or if I do know, deep down I'm scared. Just before you came in I was thinking about Mr. Blackwood. I'm afraid Thom. What if the only way back is through him? I don't want to think about it and yet I feel his presence all the time. What does he want with me anyway? I'm sure it's not because of some silly, little thing I said or did in the museum. It must be something bigger, Thom, and that's what scares me."

They both shivered as if a dark shadow had come between them and the sparkling outside world.

Thom tried to sound cheerful. "Maybe you are all wrong, Jennifer. Maybe he has forgotten about us." But something made her glance around the door and into the depths of the closet. "The calm before the storm," she muttered to herself, forgetting that Jennifer was standing right beside her.

The two of them started laughing hysterically. "Can't you imagine Mr. Blackwood scrunched up inside our cupboard, Thom?"

Thomasina squeezed her friend's hand. "You can trust me forever. And if for some reason we have to tell Benjamin our secret, I'm positive we can count on him. I know he is only a boy, but his heart isn't so terrible," she added, glancing at Jennifer.

"Who said he was terrible, Thom!"

The sound of horse's hooves coming to a stop in front of the house interrupted their conversation. They watched through the window as a man jumped down from his horse, tied the bridle to a hitching post near the gate and then rushed up the path to the front door. After the knocker had sounded a few times, a voice vibrated through the walls.

"Now he's talking through the speaking tube hanging

by the front door," Thomasina explained: "He must want Father. Remember my telling you it was for emergencies?"

"Doctor!" The voice was shaking as it called through the tube. "Can you come with me? My boy cut his leg with an axe and it's been bleeding something fierce. We're so far out of town I couldn't risk bringing him in what with all this new snow. My wife is with the boy now, holding the wound."

Thomasina was already flying down the stairs, calling back to Jennifer from the landing. "Everyone else has gone out. I know I'm supposed to be staying in this morning, but Father will need help hitching up the horse. Come quickly as you can, Jennifer. And just in case Father decides to take us along, put on every ounce of warm clothing you can find."

A few minutes later Jennifer was standing beside the cutter, holding on to the reins while Thomasina adjusted the blinkers around Old Belle's eyes. Father checked both lanterns for kerosene before finally climbing into the cutter. "Well now . . . I trust I have everything."

Thomasina looked up at him hopefully, but did not say a word.

For heaven's sake, if you want to go, do something . . . say something! Don't just stand there like a dumb idiot. Jennifer could barely restrain herself.

Father looked down at Thomasina as he snugged the buffalo rug around his feet. "You really ought to be in your room, young lady. On the other hand I could use your help. I'm certain Old Belle won't notice the difference if you two are sitting beside me and she won't tell a soul, will you Belle? Now up with you both, quickly!"

Thomasina stowed a parcel under their feet. "I just happened to be spreading some jam on Josephine's freshly baked bread," she explained. "It's still warm."

Father patted her on the head. "You are a good provider, Thomasina. Though I have a hunch what Josephine will say when she sees her crestfallen loaf."

And then they were off, skimming down the lane to the main road, past the last scattered houses until they were in the brightness of open country. As they passed the last house, which was little more than a shack, a boy waved out to them.

"Git back to yer chores," a voice yelled from the open doorway.

The boy turned away, picked up a splitting maul almost as tall as himself and brought it down with a dull thud on an upturned chunk of wood. Again and again, up—down, up—down, like some mechanical wind-up toy; until Old Belle had whisked them out of sight.

"Wasn't that Montague, the dumb kid from our class?"

"Montague? He's not the least bit stupid. You should see how he can draw! Tell Jennifer about him, Father."

"You see, Jennifer, the trouble began when Montague was little more than an infant. Apparently a neighbour found him lying half dead near the main road leading into town. When they brought him to me the poor little fellow's head was covered with bruises and both ears were bleeding. It was quite obvious that he had been punished by having his ears boxed. Of course his father denied it . . . ."

"And he had to go back home again?" Jennifer interrupted. "That's terrible. What about his mother?"

"She died when he was born." Thomasina explained.

A feeling of desolation settled around Jennifer's heart. What sort of place was this she had stumbled upon; a place where children were punished by having their ears boxed, where women died in childbirth and no one seemed particularly surprised? For once Jennifer could find nothing to say. Even with Thom sitting beside her she felt alone, an alien on a different planet. Never had she felt so homesick.

Thom must have sensed it because a moment later she said, "Mother nursed Montague back to health, you know, but his hearing was permanently damaged. I guess you have noticed how Miss Wishart is continually shouting at him?"

"She would, that old witch! If I were Montague I would have run away from home and never, ever have gone back."

"And what if there was no place to go," Father replied with a strange expression in his eyes.

For some reason Jennifer panicked. "I would have called the police. I would have asked someone for help. I mean . . . don't children have any rights?"

Thomasina was nudging her foot under the buffalo rug. Already she had said far more than she meant to. And Father was staring at her again with those all-knowing eyes of his.

Gradually, as the cold began seeping into her hands and feet, Jennifer felt the swirl of thoughts in her head slowing down. She half closed her eyes, watching the procession of elm trees on each side of the road flicking past them. If she squeezed her eyes more tightly shut she could almost be sitting in her own, familiar car, with the wildly flying telephone poles along the highway transporting her into a dizzying world somewhere between places.

Father jolted them out of their separate dream worlds with a call of encouragement to Old Belle as they descended steeply into a river valley. Jennifer watched the horse stiffen against the downward push of the cutter. Instead of open fields, spruce trees were crowding against the road which was now little more than track. When a branch jostled the side of the cutter Jennifer caught some needles and crushed them in her hand. She would know that familiar, tangy smell anywhere.

Then they were over the bridge and starting up the other side. "Come on Old Belle, up you go now girl."

Some miles later they came to a stop outside a dilapidated farmhouse. Before Jennifer could even uncurl her legs, Father had jumped down and was hurrying up the path towards the house. "Don't forget to care for Old Belle," he called back to the girls.

Gradually some feeling began to sift back into Jennifer's

legs as she hobbled after Thom who was draping a blanket over Old Belle's steaming back. With that done, they followed Father into the house.

The injured boy was lying on a sofa with a dirty rag wrapped tightly around his lower leg. Blood was still oozing from the edges. When the boy noticed the two girls standing behind the doctor he struggled to a sitting position, trying his very best to look brave. "I was cutting kindling out by the woodshed and the axe slipped. That's how I done it."

The boy lay quietly while the doctor worked, stealing an occasional glance at the girls and wincing in pain only once as the edges of the wound were drawn together. Jennifer had to force herself to watch. When the bandages were in place she felt better.

"The rags they have are too filthy to wrap around these clean bandages," Father whispered to the girls, "and I must leave them enough for next week. Now be so good as to help me."

Jennifer watched in amazement as he took off his work shirt and with Thom's help began tearing it into rags. The extra cloth they had brought along was also added to the growing pile.

Although Father had worked swiftly, it was almost dark when the farmhouse door closed behind the three of them. Old Belle welcomed them back with a whinny and a stamp of her feet. The oats which Thom had given her in a pouch hung from the harness had all been eaten. Before climbing into the cutter, Father lit the red and green lanterns attached to each side and pulled the blanket from Old Belle's back.

"Ready old girl? Off we go then. And remember there are more oats waiting for you at home."

She nuzzled Father back as if to say, don't you think I know that by now?

Father handed a parcel to Jennifer before climbing up himself. It was heavy and sort of mushy feeling. "What is it?" she asked Thom.

"Butter."

"Oh . . . so why are we hauling around a hunk of butter way out here?"

"It was the only way they could pay Father. They are a very proud family and wouldn't hear of him leaving without taking something."

Jennifer shook her head. Doctors who drive miles into the country to visit someone they have never seen before, who tear up their own shirts for outer bandages, who get paid with a chunk of butter . . . "You should see our medical clinic," she whispered over to Thomasina. But when she tried to describe it there always seemed to be a word or something that her friend couldn't understand. "We have about twenty different doctors and nurses all over the place ready to zap . . . er, I mean stick needles into you . . . "

"Needles—whatever for?" Thom interrupted. "I wouldn't care much for that!"

"You would if the needles stopped you from getting tetanus and measles and typhoid and stuff like that." Jennifer felt more than slightly superior as she watched the surprised expression growing on her friend's face. In the middle of a long explanation about how she had her tonsils out, Jennifer happened to glance over at Father. She didn't think there was any way he could hear their whispered conversation over the growing whine of the wind, but with Father you never knew for sure. "We better shut up just in case," she warned Thom.

After they fell silent, to pass the time Father began telling them about other visits he had made in the past. There was the girl with a ruptured appendix far from any hospital, the baby with whooping cough, the boy with blood poisoning caused by stepping on a rusty nail . . . the list went on and on.

Jennifer found herself listening for her own heartbeat. Had it missed a bit? Where was her pulse anyhow . . . Come to think of it she hadn't been feeling that great recently. Would it ever be scary getting sick without penicillin and all the other familiar things from the drugstore! Jennifer shivered.

As the cold settled around them, even talking became an effort. Under the buffalo rug it was warm and the wind and the bells together wove a pattern that lulled them to sleep. Even Father was overcome at last. Old Belle felt the reins going slack, she felt the snow swirling around her legs, but she kept on going until she was standing outside her own stable. Then she shook the harness bells until Mother heard them from the house.

Jennifer half woke up to the sound of Benjamin's voice and a lantern being held over her eyes. "The girls are still asleep, Father."

"Then we had best carry them into the house before we start unhitching Old Belle."

"Oh no you don't! I can walk by myself," Thomasina protested, half falling, half climbing from the cutter.

Jennifer was still too dazed to protest as she felt Benjamin lifting her and then carrying her into the house. She felt half annoyed with herself for being so weak. Somewhere in the distance Father was talking to Old Belle. "Come on, girl. You deserve a good feed of oats tonight."

6

Turning Point

After that first snowfall had covered autumn's leftovers, winter blew down on the countryside in full fury. Often at night Jennifer would lie awake listening to the wind tangling in the trees and blowing the snow into huge cornices that eventually fell with a hollow thump from the roof. Each house became an isolated kingdom, holding out against the forces of winter. Perhaps because of this Jennifer began to feel more cut off than ever from her past life. She tried to talk with Thomasina about her worries, but Thom, like the others, was becoming ever more hectic as the Christmas holidays approached. Father was rarely seen about the house since the outbreak of scarlet fever in town, while Mother and Josephine were forever fussing around in the kitchen making mincemeat, tarts, plum pudding and a hundred other surprises. Benjamin was spending every spare minute at some carpentry project which resulted in piles of sawdust outside the kitchen door, much to Josephine's disgust. Only Jennifer stood apart from the others, feeling more and more like an outsider as the Christmas season drew closer.

But moments still arrived when the loneliness and anxiety were pushed to one side: there was the sudden swoosh of sleigh runners as they spun into the river valley in search of a Christmas tree; and Archibald's triumphant laugh when he managed to "hooky-a-ride" on the back of the sleigh without anyone noticing; and the fire by the frozen river, and the skating, while Thom grumbled about having to collect firewood until she felt "bent over like Hansel and Gretel's witch"; and finally the long, twilight ride back home sitting between Benjamin and Thom, with Benjamin's scarf wrapped around her face to keep out the chill wind.

One morning after watching Mother and Josephine leave in the cutter for their weekly shopping, Jennifer sneaked into the kitchen. Good! The ashes in the woodstove were still hot from breakfast. Jennifer shoved a few more chunks of wood into the fire-box then peeked out the window again. You could never be too sure with Josephine. She had a bad habit of returning to check up on things possibly lost, stolen, or strayed, such as stray sparks from the woodstove. The coast was clear for the moment. Jennifer dashed into the pantry and scooped out some of Josephine's precious sugar from the tin standing in the corner. "She'll murder me if she finds out," Jennifer thought, as she measured the sugar into a cast iron pot. Soon the candy mixture was bubbling away on top of the stove. Even Father and Mother would approve of this Christmas present, chock full of healthy raisins and nuts. Before long Jennifer was whistling softly to herself.

Then suddenly, Christmas morning was upon them! The first thing Jennifer felt was a pair of icy hands pulling the blankets off the bed. Still only half awake, she held on to them fiercely.

"Aren't you girls ever coming?" a voice whispered from the hall. "This candle is starting to drip wax."

"I can't get her up!"

"Well hurry! Father said I could start lighting the candles on the tree."

Thom burrowed under the sheets again and grabbed one of Jennifer's feet. That did it! A few seconds later Jennifer joined the other two in the hallway. In single file they crept down the stairs, while the candle shadows plunged ahead of them into the darkness. A single snap of an electric light would send those shadows scurrying, Jennifer thought, enjoying for an instant the return of her old feelings of superiority.

Outside the parlour door Benjamin stopped to straighten his candle. Not a drop of wax must be allowed to smudge the precious rug in that room. There was just time enough for Thom to scratch her feet across the floor and touch a fiery finger to Benjamin's neck. A spark flashed in the darkness.

He turned on his sister. "If I was a measly girl I would have shrieked and the whole house would be awake by now."

"Good boy! Self-control, self-discipline, I always say."

"You beast!"

The moon was shining through the parlour window, cradling the Christmas tree in her silvery embrace. It was almost enough without the candles, but as one by one they were lit the room took on a new brilliance. The old St. Nicholas on top of the tree nodded his approval. A cobweb nearby that had managed to escape Josephine's duster danced in time to the old Saint.

But already a new day was sliding through the window and the magic was disappearing. The room was a parlour again, the cobweb had shrunk to ordinary spider size and the grownup's footsteps could be heard overhead.

"Let's peek in our stockings, quick, before they come," Thom said. "I can feel a luscious, fat orange in my heel."

"What's so special about an orange!" Jennifer shook her stocking so violently the orange bounced out and ran along the floor.

Thom crawled after it until it came to rest under the chesterfield. "Maybe it's nothing to you, Jennifer, because you seem to have had everything. But if you only got oranges once or twice a year you might think it's something special too. You needn't have been so rough." She cradled the orange in her hands.

"Mother goes to a great deal of trouble to get them," Benjamin added.

"Oh take my stinking orange," Jennifer yelled, stomping out of the room. "And take my whole stocking too. I don't want any presents."

She ran up the stairs, flying past Mother and Father without a single word and flung herself down on Thomasina's bed. She could hear them talking downstairs. Father's voice was especially clear through the floor. "We know little more about Jennifer now than we did on the day she arrived, except for the fact her home must be very different from ours. Yet I don't think that she was badly mistreated there. So why . . . why run away?" Silence for a few seconds and then Father asked abruptly, "Have you noticed how words often seem to mean something different to her than they do to us? Has she never confided in you Thomasina?"

Jennifer strained to hear the answer, but it was drowned out by the sound of kindling crackling in the parlour stove. Anyhow, Thom would never reveal the secret. It was theirs alone. But suppose Father was coming close to the truth . . . Jennifer could almost feel his all-knowing eyes gazing down upon her. Impossible! Adults could never believe anything out of the ordinary. They would say we're making up stories, going through a stage or something like that.

Jennifer heard Thomasina's footsteps starting up the stairs, until Mother's voice intervened. "We best leave the poor child by herself, Thomasina. Christmas is a difficult time for those who are lonely or carrying a burden on their shoulders."

Jennifer buried her face in the quilt. When was the last time she had really cried—was it eons ago? The wet patch under her face grew so huge she had to roll over. All that wet goose down from one bunch of tears!

Later Thomasina came upstairs carrying a sweet bun in one hand and a peeled orange in the other. "I'm sorry for sounding like such an awful prig, Jennifer. You feel so familiar I sometimes forget about our secret. I suppose you had oranges by the dozen any old day of the year and stacks of other things I've never heard of . . . ''

"As a matter of fact . . . " Jennifer was nodding her head and smiling. "But it wasn't that, Thom, not really. It was this whole Christmas business and feeling so lost, without having the foggiest idea of how to get home."

"And I guess I've been trying to push the whole idea of your leaving out of my mind. It was selfish of me, Jennifer."

"I've got to go back, Thom. There is some terrible danger for me here that gets worse the longer I stay. You have to try and understand."

"I do Jennifer, I really do. And I promise I will help, even though more than anything else in the world I wish you could stay here. Right after Christmas we'll start making plans. Perhaps . . . I mean I don't know what you think, but perhaps we should include Benjamin. And talking of Benjamin, he asked me to give you this."

Thomasina stepped aside to reveal a beautiful, handmade sled. "He made it himself, especially for you Jennifer."

"So that's where all the sawdust was coming from!" Jennifer ran her fingers over the gently curved runners. Attached to one of them was a card with the message, "To Jennifer from your trusted friend Benjamin, Christmas 1909."

Mother's voice broke in at last, calling up to them from the landing. "We should be leaving for Aunt Delight's within the hour."

Thom groaned. "Oh dear, I had forgotten all about her terrible party and I never told you either. She is a regular holy terror, Jennifer. You'll detest her. She has this gigantic house filled with everything except children, but once a year at Christmas she has to have all the little nieces and nephews over. Perhaps we could develop stomach aches and stay home."

Although she didn't get sick, Jennifer was suffering from too much good advice and a bad case of nerves by the time they reached Aunt Delight's house. Even the brass knocker on the door looked vaguely menacing as Father lifted it. A few moments later the towering figure of Aunt Delight opened the door.

"Aah, the whole family come for this most joyous occasion! So this is the new child of which you were speaking, Maude?" Aunt Delight condescended to look down upon Jennifer. "Most unusual looking," she confided to Mother in a whisper loud enough for almost everyone else to hear. "Well . . . "

Mother was making frantic gestures at Thomasina who in turn was poking Jennifer. "For goodness' sake, Jennifer, say something . . . anything!"

Jennifer managed a shaky curtsy and a mumbled "how d'you do."

Again that booming whisper! "The child's enunciation is appalling, Maude. From what sort of home must the child come?"

"My name is Jennifer in case you didn't know."

Mercifully Father broke in. "So good to see you Delight, my dear sister." He gave her a hearty bear hug which seemed to put her in a more agreeable temper for the moment.

Jennifer followed the others upstairs, after being warned by Thomasina to keep her mouth shut. When the grownups had disappeared downstairs again Thom flung her hat and coat on the guest room bed. "I hate this room! If you ask me it's haunted."

"Sleeping in such a gigantic bed would give me nightmares," Jennifer agreed. "And look at the pillow coverings, Thom."

"You mean pillow shams," Benjamin corrected her.

"Well whatever you call them, they're stupid." Below a picture of two rosy-faced children Jennifer read out the embroidered message

77

I slept and dreamt that life was beauty.
I woke and found that life was duty!

Jennifer tossed her coat over the pillows before following the others downstairs.

"It might be better if you sat between Thomasina and me," Benjamin advised her.

"Thanks, I can look after myself," Jennifer replied, though she was secretly grateful for the offer.

The other cousins were already seated at a small table near the adults. "Terrible little goody-goods!" Thom whispered to Jennifer as they sat down. "We shall probably have to sit here for hours after dinner listening to their songs and recitations. I'm glad I'm not musical."

Aunt Delight who was presiding over the main table had already begun serving vegetables to the children. Father was standing beside her carving the goose.

"She never asked me what I wanted," Jennifer protested when she saw her plate. The other children were watching her. "I hate mashed turnips. They make me puke. And she gave me a whole mound of the stuff. What'll I do with it, Thom?"

"You'll have to get rid of it somehow or she will make you sit here the rest of the afternoon. I know what—give it to Benjamin, he loves turnip. Not now though; she's looking our way."

The warning came too late. Jennifer was sliding her plate towards Benjamin who moved his elbow at the worst possible moment. The turnip flopped on to the white tablecloth. In the excitement Thomasina knocked over a glass of water which began trickling onto Jennifer's lap. The two tried to choke down their giggles.

Aunt Delight rushed over and plucked the guilty ones from the table. "What have you done!" She surveyed the flooded table, splattered with turnip. "Upstairs, both of you, until we have cleared away this bedlam."

She half dragged them upstairs. "Thomasina, you will stand inside the guest room with your back to the door, and you, child, will sit on this chair in the hall. There now, I have locked the door between you! When I think it is the proper time for you to join the others I shall come to fetch you myself."

After she had been sitting there for a few minutes Jennifer crept to the door and whispered through the keyhole. "Are you all right in there, Thom?"

"I guess so. Even a haunted room is better than being downstairs with HER! I've been reciting all the poems I know to keep my mind off ghosts and things. You better not let her catch us talking through the keyhole, Jennifer, or she'll leave us here forever."

"Who cares about that witch!" Jennifer grumbled to herself as she went back to sit down on the chair. Every so often she could hear poor old Thom talking to herself.

"Yes, Miss Darlington. Of course I can recite Tennyson's 'The Song of the Brook.' Do I have to stand up in front of the whole class?

I come from haunts of coot and tern
I make a sudden sally,
And sparkle out among the fern,
To . . . um . . . BICKER down a valley . . .
What does bicker mean? Um . . . how the river flows
. . . Yes, Miss Darlington, I shall look up the difficult words in future.

I chatter chatter as I flow
To join the brimming river . . .

To help pass the time Jennifer started sorting through the junk in her pocket; there was the handkerchief Mother had given her, a rumpled note from Benjamin . . . her glance fell on the twenty-five cent piece that she always carried around. She forgot about Aunt Delight and her rotten party; she even forgot about Thomasina on the other side of the door. When are you going to take us back home, old quarter? I bet you get homesick too, sometimes, especially like now . . . Do you think Mom and Dad are missing me as much as I miss them? I wish I knew what they were doing this very second. Maybe it's like flying around the world in a super-fast jet; maybe they are asleep in the middle of the night somewhere . . . maybe . . . wherever you are, "Hello," Jennifer finished weakly. She shivered, suddenly feeling dizzy.

She stood up. "Listen, I've got to get out of here. It's been too long. What if I start forgetting what it's like back there . . ."

Outside the guest room door Jennifer paused for a moment. If only there was an extra key lying around. There was no point telling Thom she was sneaking away. She would only worry more, shut away in that dreadful room. Besides, what she didn't know the others couldn't blame her for.

As Jennifer crept down the stairs she could hear the goody-good children singing in the distance. Perfect! It drowned out the creaking of the stairs. Jennifer was almost out the door when she remembered that her coat was still locked away upstairs with Thom. Reaching back inside she dragged one of the cousin's coats off the rack. That would make Aunt Delight furious! When the door was safely closed behind her, Jennifer stopped to take a deep breath of fresh air. Foggy though it was outside, it was a hundred times better than being cooped up inside that house. Poor Thom, though. Jennifer could not help feeling a twinge of guilt at the thought of her friend locked away in that haunted room. She had slipped away without even a whispered good-bye.

The roads were almost deserted with the oncoming darkness of that mid-winter afternoon. Besides it was Christmas day and everyone else would be with friends or family. Only she was alone. Jennifer squeezed the twenty-five cent piece in her hand. It gave her enough courage to go on. For a while she wandered down the main street of town, looking into shop windows that only a few days before had been alive with Christmas decorations. They were now dark and silent. Jennifer quickened her steps, then ducked into a doorway to avoid meeting a lone figure who was moving in her direction. After it had passed she continued on her way. In the deepening fog and darkness she was no longer sure where she was, so it was with some surprise that she found herself standing at the main crossroads. A signpost loomed above her. Jennifer waited for something to appear on the road, something that would transport her away, choose a direction for her. But the only sound was the occasional plop of melting snow from the signpost. After what seemed ages, Jennifer turned abruptly in the direction of the railway station.

The building was familiar because she had been there once before with Thomasina and Benjamin. Thom had told her that trains ran east to Toronto every day. The city! Even the name sounded exciting to Jennifer, a link with the world that seemed to be slowly slipping away from her. "What's the use," Jennifer reminded herself. "It isn't my city; it's the place where Thomasina and Benjamin's grandparents live. I don't live there anymore . . . we can locate no family of that surname presently residing in Toronto . . . '' Those words still echoed in Jennifer's ears. Still, if she could find one familiar thing—a street, a building, a park . . . Could that be the link between her worlds? Jennifer felt her hands shaking.

The station looked deserted except for a single lantern shining from one window. Jennifer rubbed her sleeve across the damp window until she could see inside. The station agent was bent over a desk filing away his books and papers for the day. Jennifer rapped on the door.

"Come in, come in. Don't stand there with the door open and the cold blowing in."

Jennifer stepped inside, grateful for the warmth coming from the one small stove. She hesitated for a moment before asking, "I was just wondering about trains going to the east . . . " Her voice trailed off, sounding hollow in that empty room.

"No further trains this afternoon or evening. First one

81

from the west arrives tomorrow morning, 8 a.m., leaves again 8:15 sharp.'' He leaned back in his chair and inspected Jennifer. "Now why's a young thing like yourself wanderin' around alone on Christmas day? Don't you belong anywhere? Come to think of it, I don't believe I've seen your face before in these parts.''

Jennifer began backing away towards the door. "Sorry for disturbing you as you were trying to close up,'' she mumbled. "I'm pretty late myself. Guess I better be getting home.''

"Wait—don't rush off! Take this.'' The station agent tried to hand her a train schedule, but Jennifer was already out the door and running down the platform.

"Damn this fog and everything!'' Jennifer came to an abrupt halt at the end of the railway platform. In her rush to escape the prying station agent she had taken a wrong turn. The way out was in the opposite direction. "And I haven't got much time left,'' she muttered. "I bet anything they're looking for me.''

Jennifer peered ahead into the darkness. There were only the empty tracks disappearing into the fog. Was she imagining things or did she hear a slight sound from up ahead? But the agent said the last train had gone by. Nobody in his right mind would be out in such weather . . . The fog seemed to stifle her thoughts, the very words inside her throat. "Thom . . . Benjamin!'' she wanted to scream out. The sound was almost beside her now. Jennifer spun around and began racing down the platform. Faster and faster! Her footsteps seemed to be echoing after her and behind them was something dark, menacing and unknown.

A light appeared ahead. Jennifer stumbled into the main street and collapsed on a bench in front of the station. She wiped her forehead which was streaming with perspiration. "I feel awful.'' A shiver ran through her body and a few minutes later she was shaking violently all over. What if I'm getting sick! I can't—not here. She felt her forehead. It was burning hot.

Jennifer dragged herself up from the bench and along the road leading back to the signpost. She hadn't gone very far when she heard horses' hooves and a man shouting "Whuu-up there!"

With her feet rooted to the spot as if in a dream, Jennifer watched the daily coach hurtle past in a burst of light and noise. Then it was gone, sucking the fog behind in little clouds that fell back helpless at her feet. Somehow the last link with her other world seemed to have been broken. "Don't be silly," she told herself, "it was only a coach like all the others passing through town."

Jennifer forced herself to keep going. I can't get sick, not now. Remember they don't have penicillin or any of those other pills to make you better. Who's that ahead of me there on the road? Nobody . . . I guess it must be the fog making me dizzy. "Oh Thom . . . and Benjamin too, please come and help me . . . I feel so dreadfully sick."

Somehow Jennifer managed to stumble up the pathway leading to their house. It was completely dark and the kitchen door was bolted shut. Pushing her way into the woodshed, Jennifer found a pile of old vegetable sacks which she pulled over herself. A few minutes later she was asleep.   *   *   *

Was it hours later or only a moment? Jennifer became aware of voices close by. "I hope she is safe at home here and hasn't taken it into her head to run away again," Father said.

"Jennifer wouldn't run away, not without telling me first," Thomasina insisted.

"Jennifer . . . Jennifer . . . " Mother's voice filled the empty house.

Thom called from upstairs. "She isn't in our bedroom or anywhere else."

Jennifer felt a cool hand on her forehead. She struggled to say something, but couldn't. Benjamin's voice sounded very far away as he kneeled down to pick her up. "Jennifer . . . Jennifer, why didn't you tell Thomasina where you were going? We've been hunting . . . I was so worried you had gone. Don't you care for us?''

Bright lights were shining down on her eyes. "Shall I prepare a mustard bath?'' Mother asked.

"I fear she is too ill, Maude. The child is half delirious with fever.''

"Is . . . is it terribly serious Father?'' Benjamin was looking down at her again.

"If you two would only move away from the couch and give me enough space to examine the patient!''

While Father was looking for something in his medicine chest, Thomasina crept back to her friend's side. Jennifer wanted to say something; she tried to move her lips. "But Mom . . . I promised this new friend of mine that we'd go to a movie together. I don't want to go to the museum again. And she is my very best friend. Her name is . . . it's . . . wait a minute, I can't seem to remember. Thomasina! That's who she is.''

Thom whispered in her ear, "Of course I'm your friend, Jennifer and you're going to be better soon.''

"Thomasina!'' Father was standing over her. "I thought I warned you and Benjamin about coming too close. What if she has scarlet fever or some other contagious disease?''

"I was just trying to comfort Jennifer. Besides I'm too tough for ordinary, everyday diseases.''

Father smiled. "Then I could certainly use a miracle worker like you. At any rate she has none of the colour and rash of scarlet fever.'' Jennifer felt him listening to her chest. "But she does have pneumonia, a severe case I am afraid.''

"Will . . . will she get better soon, Father?'' Benjamin asked.

"Time alone will tell, my dear children. She has probably been ill for several days without our even realizing it. Possibly the turning point will come tonight and by morning . . . Other than watching and waiting there is little more we can do to help.''

"We want to watch over her tonight, Father."

"No, Thomasina, you and Benjamin must get your sleep. Mother and I shall take turns here. Now off to bed with you."

Jennifer was vaguely aware of Thom grumbling to Benjamin as they shuffled slowly out of the room. "You know Benjamin, the trouble with grownups is that they never will believe anyone else is grownup. It doesn't make sense. How can they expect us to sleep properly tonight when Jennifer is so sick?"

Jennifer wanted to call out, "No, don't go," but she couldn't move or speak. Far, far in the distance she could hear Mother singing one of her favourite hymns:

Like a little candle
Burning in the night . . .
You in your small corner,
And I in mine

She felt Father wiping her forehead with a damp cloth and removing the blanket which was so heavy on her chest. Afterwards he sat down at his desk in the corner of the room.

Gradually the house grew still except for the grandfather clock in the hallway chiming out the quarter hours. Jennifer stirred once or twice on the couch. Was she awake or was she dreaming? Figures were streaming past the couch in an endless procession; Montague, Miss Wishart, Josephine, Archibald . . . And always as they passed in front of her they paused for an instant. "Seen and Not Heard Children," they were chanting, "Seen and Not Heard Children. Who do you think you are? Intruder . . . intruder . . . " Like a pack of cards the figures flicked past her, faster and faster, before finally collapsing in a heap on the ground.

Jennifer struggled to lift her head from the pillow. The office door was creaking open. A shoe snaked through and a gloved hand widened the crack. There was something terribly familiar about that hand. It was carrying a camera. Jennifer shut her eyes in terror.

"Mr. Blackwood!" But no sound came from the cry on her lips.

Father was slumped over in his office chair, sound asleep. The dark shadow slipped past him towards the couch where Jennifer was lying. Slowly he began unfolding his camera, all the while talking to himself, or was it partly to Jennifer? "Not the best conditions for my work, but then my camera is unique. Now if I can draw closer without disturbing the others in the house. Meddlers they are, especially the girl and the boy. They seem to believe they have some life of their own apart from me. Well I shall deal with them in time! Just one more close-up before I can claim her for my precious collection. And what an addition that will be! In comparison these others here will be as faded nothings."

His gloved hands slid the camera soundlessly across the floor towards Jennifer, closer and closer . . .

The office door was flung open. "Jennifer!" Thom's voice rang out. "Look at me, beyond the dark shadow. It's me . . . Thomasina. I'm here."

The darkness dissolved and Jennifer found herself staring into her friend's face. "Lucky . . . you were just in time Thom . . . " and then her eyes flickered shut.

Father came rushing towards the couch. "What on earth are you doing here, Thomasina!"

"A noise or something woke me up. Perhaps it was a dream, but Jennifer seemed to be calling out to us."

Father passed his hands over his forehead, "Strange that we both were affected. Such a nightmare I was having! I swear its dark presence is lingering here yet."

Benjamin's and then Mother's footsteps came hurrying down the stairs. "Is she all right, Father? Oh Thom, I'm so sorry; I fell asleep by mistake."

"Never mind, so did I, at least for a while."

Jennifer felt Father's hand on her forehead. "Hmm, much cooler and her pulse rate is slower. If we are lucky she may be over the crisis."

"Thank heavens!" Mother sighed. "I was praying for morning. I shall go and make some hot cocoa for us all."

7

Once Upon a Time

At first Jennifer lay in bed only half aware of the constant comings and goings around her—Thomasina sitting on the edge of the bed, Josephine sailing in with endless trays of "drink-up-nows," Mother singing hymns, Father taking her temperature, Benjamin bearing gifts and once a get-well poem . . . Sometimes she felt so sick that even these dim shadows faded into a more elemental world of light and darkness. Had there ever been another time in another place, long before her illness? If so it was peopled by shadows even fainter than those flitting around her now.

But gradually the outside world began to return. At first it was the square of light that was her window on the opposite side of the room. The snow and then the rain pelted against it, the moon ran races with the sun across it, a maple branch tickled it. One day the gigantic icicle that had hung there for ages was gone. The sun was shining and a crow was cawing and strutting on the maple branch.

One Sunday morning before the family left for church, Benjamin came tiptoeing into Jennifer's room and opened the small drawer in the chest beside her bed. Still half asleep, Jennifer watched him through a slit in one eye. He hurriedly stuffed something inside the drawer, but as he was closing it again stopped and gave a low whistle. A metallic sounding object clinked against the thermometer case. For an instant he gazed down at Jennifer, then turned and hurried from the room. Jennifer heard him calling to Thomasina and afterwards the two of them were whispering together in the hallway.

"If you would give me a chance to open my mouth perhaps I could explain," Thom was protesting.

"Explain—ha! A strange coin with a picture of a queen who is most certainly not our Queen Victoria . . . and 1981 written on it. Yes, what does it mean, Thom? Or is someone playing a trick? But come to think of it when I look back . . . Jennifer's sudden arrival, her strange appearance and behaviour, perhaps it does add up to something. Yes by all means Thomasina, go ahead and explain this if you can."

"Benjamin, for goodness sake will you please SHUT UP! Do show some self-control," she mimicked Miss Wishart's voice.

"Self-control . . . with this mystery staring me in the face?"

"Not so loud, Benjamin; there are too many ears around this house." Thom glanced downstairs where Mother and Father were waiting near the front door. "I promise you we shall talk about it after church. Anyhow we're late now and I can't find my silly hat. Did you touch it, Benjamin?"

"Don't go changing the subject, Thomasina. I know you. All right, after church then . . . you promise."

"Of course I do. Now stop pestering me." Thom waited until he had gone before rushing into Jennifer's room. "I can't stay. Everyone is waiting for me downstairs. But I have to tell you. Benjamin found your twenty-five cent piece in the drawer. Don't ask me why he was meddling around there in the first place. Now he is all suspicious and he made me promise to explain everything after church this morning. Jennifer, I think we have to tell him the truth. What do you say?"

Jennifer, now thoroughly awake, sat up in bed. "Simmer down, Thom. I can hardly understand a word you are saying. No wonder Benjamin is suspicious. You sound like a mini-detective or something."

"I said Benjamin found your twenty-five cent piece, so do we tell him everything or not?"

"Oh sure—tell him all the gory details! Thom, please stop talking in riddles, tell him what?"

"About you of course, where you come from and . . ."

"Great, really great . . . Once upon a time there was a kid called Jennifer and she lived with her family in a big house near the edge of town . . . Thom, as I've been trying to tell you, maybe a hundred times, I can't remember things properly from the time before I was sick. But you never will listen; you keep changing the subject as if you don't want to hear me. I've been trying, Thom, honestly I have."

Thomasina was staring at her friend. "Are you sure you're feeling all right, Jennifer? I could call Father."

"Of course I'm all right. I feel better today than I have for ages. And Mother told me yesterday that I can go back to school soon. Isn't that great?"

Thomasina was shaking her head and muttering to herself as she hurried from the room. "How could I have missed all those signs . . . her not talking about home anymore or going back . . ."

After Thomasina had left, Jennifer rolled over in bed and opened the drawer. What had Benjamin been doing anyhow messing around in there! Those two had been acting so strangely recently, especially Thom who wasn't making any sense at all. She pulled out the box that Benjamin had stuffed in the drawer. It was full of lozenges. Jennifer smiled to herself, picked out a heart-shaped lozenge with the words "Be Mine" printed across it in bold letters and popped it into her mouth. As she was putting the box back, her fingers brushed against the coin in the bottom of the drawer. Out of curiosity she picked the twenty-five cent piece up. There was something familiar about the shape and the way it felt between her fingers. Jennifer placed the coin in the middle of her forehead and lay back on her pillow, thinking.

Later on Jennifer heard the family returning from church and Thom climbing the stairs in her Sunday morning "one-step-at-a-time" manner.

"What a bore!" Thom exclaimed as she flopped down on the bed. "You were lucky you had to stay here. The sermon droned on and on as usual and Father fell asleep again. And for the hundredth time old Mrs. Cook was complaining about us driving our horses on a Sunday . . . 'the Lord doesn't want His creatures to be worked on the Sabbath . . . ' So what are we going to do with the rest of our boring Sunday? Any clever ideas? I bet you used to have more fun than us."

Jennifer held up the twenty-five cent piece. "Perhaps for a start we could talk about this."

Thomasina hesitated. It was just what she didn't want to talk about at the moment. They had been talking about that coin all the way home from church; ever since making an excuse to get away from the grownups. At first Benjamin had refused to believe the story. "It's not sensible or logical or . . . or anything," he fumed. But gradually as she went on it seemed to become the only possible answer to so many nagging questions. "All right, Thom," he said finally, "presuming that your story is true, I really don't see how we can help Jennifer if she has forgotten her home. It would be better for her to stay with us." She tried to make him see how dangerous that could be. Either he couldn't or didn't want to understand; not that she could really blame him.

Thomasina was still hesitating. Perhaps it would be better not to upset Jennifer while she was still recovering. Perhaps Benjamin was right about her staying on, at least for the time being. And since there had been no signs of Mr. Blackwood recently, surely it couldn't be that dangerous. In a few weeks or so, starting with the little things, she could gradually remind Jennifer of her past . . . time enough later . . .

"Thom . . . " Jennifer was waving the twenty-five cent piece in front of her friend's face. "I asked you a question and you seem to be miles away."

"Uuuh? Oh sorry, Jennifer. I was busy thinking about something. Jennifer?"

"Yes, Thom?"

"Do you remember anything at all from the time before your illness? I mean way back, not just a few days or weeks . . . "

"I honestly don't know, Thom. Sometimes I think I do, at other times everything seems so hazy. When I hold this coin for instance I feel a whole batch of familiar feelings. Or I'll say a certain word and that word keeps echoing in my ears as though it were bouncing back from somewhere else."

"You know, Father said something once about people losing their memory for a while after an accident or illness. It's got some funny name . . . but I've forgotten."

"Amnesia."

"How did you know?" Thomasina looked surprised.

"Oh I don't know. While you were talking the word sort of popped into my head. Just so long as they don't shut me up in the nut-house, who cares," Jennifer joked.

But Thomasina was looking very serious. "We won't say anything to Mother and Father for the time being. And about that twenty-five cent piece, Jennifer, keep it in a safe place and don't show it to a soul. I have a suspicion it may be more important than any of us realize . . . Now have some rest while I go downstairs to help Mother."

Jennifer lay back. What Thom had said made her more confused than ever. But there was no hurry. As soon as she was feeling better it would be easy to figure everything out.

8
Changeovers

As if in tune with the lengthening days Jennifer felt her own strength increasing. Every afternoon now she exercised in the garden. She watched the last sooty pile of snow disappear and the first dazzling primula appear. And then, miraculously, Father said she could go back to school. She was better!

One morning as they were getting ready for school Thom drew Jennifer aside. "Listen, I'm sick and tired of the way Archibald is always ambushing us. I have a hunch he will be lying in wait for us again this morning, but this time I've got a surprise for our friend Mr. Archibald. Look in the bag here."

"Bits of potato, so what Thom!"

"Wait a minute, Jennifer, these potato pieces are special. I rubbed them all over my warts to make sure they are covered with fresh wart germs . . . Oh, oh, here comes Josephine to nag us, let's get going."

Once they were safely out the front door Thom continued. "Then when Archibald comes leaping out at us we drop the wart bag and run. Thinking there must be something luscious inside, he opens the bag and, ha . . . ha . . . this is the good part, he catches all my juicy warts."

"If you believe all that stuff about catching wart germs," Jennifer said dubiously. "It doesn't sound very scientific to me. Say, isn't that Archibald's foot sticking out from Mr. Macklin's hedge?"

"Yaa—hoo!" In spite of being prepared they both jumped

when Archibald sprang from the hedge. Thomasina dropped the bag, stumbled as if she was trying to pick it up, then ran on.

"I've got your bag," Archibald yelled triumphantly.

"Give it back to Thom, you little creep."

"Phooey! I'm opening it up." Puzzled at finding only potatoes, Archibald dumped the whole mess on the ground. "Why you little cheats! There's nothing except a bunch of withered up potatoes."

"Oh, but there's lots more," Jennifer crowed. "You tell him, Thom."

"I rubbed the potatoes on my warts, so now they are creeping with wart germs."

"Archibald has warts, Archibald has warts . . . " the two of them were chanting.

"Wait till I get my hands on you rotten girls!" Archibald pelted them with potatoes as they dashed off. "You're going to catch it, just wait until after school."

At recess Archibald came sauntering up to them. "I wager you two are scared silly. And don't think you can escape from me either—I'm the fastest runner around here."

"Oh yeah?" Jennifer took a step towards Archibald. When she really stretched she was a shade taller than he was. "You want to make a bet on that?"

"Of course! I can run circles around any sissy girl."

As the argument grew hotter a crowd gathered around them. Finally Benjamin broke through and pushed the two apart. "What's going on here?"

"Ask your stupid friend there!" Jennifer replied sullenly. "All he can do is boast about how fast a runner he is."

"Ask your sweet, little sister," Archibald shouted.

"So you're at the bottom of this, Thomasina! I might have known."

"Who said that!" Thom shouted back at her brother. "Anyhow, maybe I have a way to settle this whole matter. Why don't Jennifer and Archibald challenge each other to a race at lunch time today, down by the poplar grove?"

"And naturally the best man will win," Archibald smirked.

"You'll be eating those words in my dust clouds," Jennifer promised.

When the bell rang to end recess, Benjamin hurried after Jennifer. "Don't go in that race," he begged her. "It's another of Thomasina's hare-brained schemes. Archibald is by far the best runner in the school and you might hurt yourself trying to race against him. Remember you have been sick."

"That was ages ago," Jennifer replied scornfully. "Besides I've been exercising every day. You just think girls shouldn't run against boys, their muscles are too flabby and everything, right?"

"No, I never said that, Jennifer. Why are you so suspicious of me?"

"Because I'm so mad at that stuffed-up friend of yours, that's why." She turned to face Benjamin. "I'm sorry. It's none of your fault. But wish me luck in the race. I guess I'll need it."

There was already a crowd gathered by the poplar grove when Jennifer and Thomasina hurried from school. It was just like Miss Wishart to have kept them in at such a crucial moment.

"I'm worried about running in this skirt," Jennifer said.

"Well, what else could you wear?"

"I'm not sure. All I know is that this skirt feels rotten flapping around my legs."

Archibald had caught sight of his rival. "Seeing as you are just a girl how about me giving you a head start to make everything fair and square?"

"Head start? Ha! You better start saying your prayers." Jennifer took her place beside Archibald at the starting line and began doing some limbering up exercises.

"What do you think you're trying to do?" Archibald asked, after watching her out of the corner of his eye for several minutes.

"Loosening my muscles, getting warmed up before the race starts, so I won't have a muscle cramp."

"Never seen anyone doing that before," he grumbled. "Anyhow boys don't get cramps. That's girl stuff."

But when Jennifer glanced sideways a moment later Archibald was bent over rubbing his legs. She laughed to herself. Even if she didn't win it was good to see him getting nervous.

Thom had finally managed to untangle the cord that she had scrounged from the principal's office. With Benjamin holding the other end she stretched it across the finish line. "Everybody ready?" she called out.

"No, wait a second," Jennifer replied. "I've got to fix this dumb skirt." Jennifer wrenched it so hard the snaps broke and the skirt crumpled to the ground.

A gasp of horror went up from the crowd and then someone sniggered, "Look at her bloomers, will you!"

"Let 'em laugh," Jennifer fumed, as she stomped out of her skirt. "It won't stop the race and at least I can run properly now."

Archibald giggled and started to say something.

"Shut up," Jennifer snapped, not waiting for him to finish. "Ready!" she yelled back to Thom.

"All right then . . . On your mark, get ready. GO!"

Jennifer sprang into the lead with her professional racing start, but Archibald soon closed the gap between them. First one, then the other, pulled ahead. Jennifer felt her throat going raspy and dry. She could not seem to shake that persistent figure glued to her side. It seemed to have become a part of her own laboured breathing. The finish line was flashing ahead. With a tremendous lunge that almost split her chest, Jennifer sprawled across the line a fraction ahead of Archibald.

"Grab your skirt, wrap it around yourself . . . do anything," Thom warned, "or we'll be in desperate trouble. Here comes that old witch, Miss Wishart."

The race changed everything. Jennifer felt she had earned a certain respect from her classmates. Even Archibald managed a grudging "hello" now and again.

9

Fortune Teller

From the dried skeletons of elm trees that fringed the roads and lined each field, a lace of green was appearing. A few days later a full canopy of leaves had sprung forth from the branches. Everywhere new things were bursting out: clover from the brownness of last year's hay field, watercress along the river valley, tadpoles with too-soon legs in the melt water pools, young lambs . . . Spring had surely arrived.

"Everything but us is changing," Thomasina grumbled, looking at her reflection in the mirror. "Trees are lucky, they get something fresh each year, but we have to make do with the same pale, leftover winter face." She squinted her eyes at the reflection.

Jennifer was staring aimlessly out the kitchen window, a habit that seemed to have grown since her illness. Though miles away in thought she had still heard Thom. "The worst thing is having to wear our winter clothes in this boiling hot weather. I feel like a turtle that needs to shed its old shell."

"Turtles indeed!" Josephine sniffed with the hint of a smile on her face. "I have listened to enough complaining for one day. You know very well we only change into summer clothes on the twenty-fourth of May. Now you two skedaddle out of my kitchen before you are late for school."

Somehow Miss Wishart was managing to drone away the month of May, but the warm sounds coming from outside the classroom window were gradually becoming too distracting. It was obvious the pupils needed to be taught a lesson. When Montague arrived at school for the third time in a row without any shoes, it was the proverbial "straw that broke the camel's back." He was soundly strapped in spite of his protests.

"Some fellow threw my boots into the creek. I saw them floating away downstream, before they got drowned someplace. My Pa is still livid. Says we ain't got the wherewithal to buy new ones."

When Father heard this story he was so angry he left his office and marched down to school, carrying an extra pair of boots that Mother had found in the woodshed.

"A mite squeaky about the toes," Montague whimpered gratefully, wiping a drippy nose on his sleeve, "but I'll make do with 'em."

After this, matters got even more out of hand in the classroom. Jennifer and Thomasina were separated for creating a disturbance and as punishment had to sit beside a boy. That experiment ended with a howl, when Thom on a dare, slipped a tack under Archibald's behind. Thomasina was sent from the class in disgrace, but Miss Wishart didn't dare to punish her any further for fear of her father.

But with Montague it was a different matter. One particularly noisy afternoon he ended up sitting in the corner of the classroom wearing a paper dunce hat that Miss Wishart had ordered him to make. DUNCE was scrawled across the front in bright red letters.

When Jennifer saw him sitting there alone on the stool, fighting back tears, she exploded. She knew what would happen. The three-thirty bell had gone so most of the pupils had left. But poor Montague would have to go on sitting there with that ridiculous hat perched on his head until Miss Wishart would say very slowly, relishing each word, "You may leave now Montague. Let us hope that you have learned your lesson once and for all. The devil always manages to find work for idle hands . . . " Then Montague would arrive home late to face yet another licking from his Pa.

Jennifer yanked the hat off Montague's head and stomped on it. Right under Miss Wishart's unbelieving stare, she dragged Montague from the classroom.

"I can't understand why she let you go," Thomasina said on the way home. "You walked out cool as a cucumber."

"She was probably too stunned to move."

"But how did you find the nerve, Jennifer?"

"I couldn't stand it anymore. Did you see Montague's face all wizened up like a dried apple? Is she ever sadistic!"

"I guess a teacher wouldn't do that sort of thing where you come from, eh Jennifer?" As usual Thom was trying to make her remember.

"Of course not . . ." Jennifer started to say, then floundered around for an explanation.

Thom waited patiently for the reply.

"For the umpteenth time I'm sorry, Thom. I knew what I wanted to say when I started."

"Never mind. If it's really important to you it will come back eventually. And anyhow we don't have to worry about teachers or dunce hats tomorrow, because as everyone knows," and Thomasina burst out singing:

Oh the twenty-fourth of May
Is the Queen's birthday,
And if you don't give us a holiday
We'll all run away.

At breakfast the next morning Thomasina was so exultant over her new summer clothes that she had little time for eating. "They feel like feathers, like the down on a baby chick. Why do we always have to wait until the twenty-fourth of May? It's been summery feeling for ages."

"Well, this new collar is still bothering me," Jennifer grumbled. She looked at the picture of Queen Victoria looming over them. "I bet it's all your fault!"

"Don't let Josephine catch you talking about Queen Victoria like that."

98

"If you girls would only eat your breakfast," Benjamin interrupted, "and think about more important things than clothes. Complain, complain . . . and the circus will be starting any moment now."

"You would complain too if you had to put up with our clothes," Thomasina insisted.

Benjamin thumped his porridge bowl down on the table. "I'm leaving now, with or without you two."

"For goodness' sake," Thom spluttered through a mouthful of porridge. "You needn't be so huffy-puffy. We're coming."

The whole town was in a holiday mood. From every window and street corner flags were flying, some as large as tablecloths, others the size of small handkerchiefs. Mr. Purdy was standing by his storefront, waving at the crowds and handing out red, white and blue gumdrops to all the children. In the town square the band was thumping out a steady stream of marching music.

Even from a distance Jennifer could feel the excitement of the circus. She wrinkled her nose a bit, like a pleased rabbit hopping towards a lettuce patch. There was an indescribable smell in the air of animals, food cooking, dust, sun lingering on tent roofs, all mixed with the scent of growing things pressing in from the surrounding countryside. Inside the circus grounds the noise and confusion of voices was overpowering—"Try your luck in the shooting gallery; step right up and see the fabulous bearded woman; ice cream cones, one copper; choose a fiery steed for a ride on the world famous carousel . . . "

Benjamin ploughed straight ahead towards the largest tent where the main show was just starting. The three of them found some empty seats behind an enormously fat woman and her equally fat children. The sun beat down steadily against the tent roof as act after act passed through the ring: clowns, acrobats, trained bear, fire-eater . . . The fat children began to squirm about on their bench like pats of melting butter. Jennifer had to keep twisting from side to side in order to see past them. By the time the highlight of the show, the famous elephant troupe, appeared, even Benjamin was growing weary.

As they were leaving the tent a crowd jostling to get inside for the next show momentarily separated Jennifer from the other two. "Care to have your fortune told, dearie?" a voice cackled in her ear. "Step right inside my tent here and look into my crystal ball." An old woman was gripping her arm with incredible force.

"I don't have time. Let go of my arm, it's hurting. Please!" Jennifer tried to wrench herself free.

"Takes only a moment, my pretty child."

"I'm not your pretty child and for the last time I don't want my fortune told . . ." Why was that voice so familiar sounding? "Thom . . . Benjamin . . ." she called out desperately now. "Where are you?"

But they were already lost in the crowds and the strange force of that fortune teller's voice was drawing Jennifer into the depths of the tent where the crystal ball was resting on a table.

"Sit down, my child." The old woman drew the black shawl she was wearing more tightly about her head. "Now you wouldn't happen to have a coin? New, old—it matters not."

Reluctantly, Jennifer felt herself drawing out the twenty-five cent piece from the bottom of her purse. Thomasina's warning about keeping the coin in a safe place was echoing in her ears. "This is the last thing I have left," Jennifer heard herself saying, without knowing exactly what she meant.

"Ah, I know that, my child, but it is the very thing I need." The old woman held up the coin in the dim light, chuckled to herself and then popped the piece of silver under the dark globe.

"You have to give it back to me afterwards. It's very precious you know."

"That I know, dearie . . . Now look deeply into my

crystal ball and I shall see what the future holds. Aah . . . it grows dim, the meagre light flickers. But I can see how swiftly time flies, like the leaves filtering down from the trees in fall or the dry grass blowing before the wind. How quickly your year here is drawing to an end and how soon memory dims, leaving only a faded picture of what once was. And when the year has ended the others shall disappear leaving behind the solitary child lost in time. Where shall she go . . . what shall she do?''

The dark globe was growing larger. Jennifer could no longer see her reflection in it, but only an emptiness that spun endlessly round and round. Where were the other two? Weren't they looking for her? ''Thomasina . . . Benjamin!'' Although her arm felt as if a weight were pressing down on it, she managed to sweep her hand across the table and in doing so sent the globe crashing to the floor. It splintered into a thousand pieces.

The fortune teller moved towards her threateningly. ''You will come to rue your wayward actions!''

''Jennifer!'' It was Benjamin's voice calling to her from somewhere outside the tent. ''Where are you?''

''Here . . . oh hurry. I'm caught in here.''

Benjamin burst into the tent. ''Jennifer! What's wrong? I can hardly see in this dim light.'' He caught her by the arm. ''Tell me, is anyone else here? Were they harming you? If so . . . '' He clenched his fist.

Thom pushed her way past the tent flap. ''Are you there? I can't see a thing.''

''It's all right, Thom. I've found Jennifer. Something terrible must have happened, though. She is shaking like a leaf.''

''But she was standing right where Benjamin is,'' Jennifer finally managed to stutter. ''The fortune teller, I mean ⋅ . . . You've got to believe me. And she stole my coin, my precious coin. Unless . . . maybe it fell on the floor with the crystal ball.''

Jennifer crumpled to her knees on the ground, searching

for the lost twenty-five cent piece. "I knew I was to look after it, not show it to a soul and now look what I've gone and done. What's wrong with me anyhow . . . ''

Thomasina stared at Benjamin. "It was him—I know. It was Mr. Blackwood. And he needs that coin so Jennifer will be in his power . . . I'm sure. And what about us? I fear we may all be in some danger now.''

Benjamin forced himself to laugh. "You girls! You are always imagining something. A half-witted old fortune teller drags Jennifer in here and immediately it becomes Mr. Blackwood up to some evil deed. Mr. Blackwood indeed! I've never seen the fellow. How do I know he isn't just another figment of your overactive imagination, Thomasina? Besides, I'm old enough to protect us from anything or anybody . . . ''

Now it was Thom's turn to shake her head. "You can be so stubborn, Benjamin. Can't you see how helpless she is since losing her memory? All right, close your silly eyes to the danger, but I don't intend to sit around forever, doing nothing.''

Jennifer gave a sudden cry and stood up. "I've found it. But I also cut myself on that glass from the crystal ball.''

Thom breathed a sigh of relief. "Well thank goodness for small mercies, as Josephine would say. Let's see that cut. Hmm, it's quite deep. I think we better have Father look at it when we get home in case there is any glass caught inside.''

Thom glanced nervously around the tent. "Meanwhile let's get out of here before anything else happens. You'll have to tell us the absolutely whole story, Jennifer.''

After the dim light inside the tent it was almost blinding in the open air. They wandered around the circus for a while until the heat and the crowds became so stifling that even Benjamin felt ready to leave. A gigantic thunderhead was slowly blotting out the sun.

"If we want to beat the storm we ought to be leaving right away,'' Benjamin warned.

"I vote for home," Thom shivered. Somehow the presence of the fortune teller, whoever she might be, had darkened the rest of the afternoon.

As they hurried along the road, they kept glancing backwards to keep track of the storm's progress. Before long the thunderhead had claimed the whole sky. A breeze began to stir the trees along the road, spinning the leaves around until their pale undersides were showing. Somewhere, not far behind them, a flash of lightning hit the ground and the thunder growled its anger. A single drop of rain came down, then another.

Thomasina was still looking anxiously over her shoulder. "It's coming too fast for us to outrun. What if a tornado came bowling down on us from those clouds? We ought to take shelter."

Jennifer squinched her eyes at the clouds. "The chances of being hit by lightning are just about zero, Thom. Why not relax and enjoy the feel of the wind and rain on your face? It's way cooler now."

"And tornadoes are rare in these parts," Benjamin added scientifically. "You've been reading too many of those fantasy books of yours, Thomasina."

Another crack of thunder, almost at their heels, sent the three of them racing towards a nearby barn. They squeezed through a crack in the loft doors as the storm broke over their heads.

"For two people who aren't worried about storms you followed me awfully quickly," Thom observed.

Jennifer grinned. "No point in getting wet, was there?"

One section of the loft was still filled with hay left over from the previous season. Jennifer took one look at it and began climbing the long ladder that led to the top. With a yell she jumped off and plunged deep, deep into the hay below. Thomasina started after her.

"Better not," Benjamin warned, "if the farmer catches us he will be furious."

"You're just a scaredy-cat," Thom retorted, already half way up.

"Drat you terrible girls!" Benjamin grumbled. "You're always making trouble for me. Why can't you be like other girls for a change?"

Jennifer watched his slow progress up the ladder. Poor fellow, he was obviously scared stiff. It must be dreadful with two girls watching. For once she didn't feel like crowing out her superiority. "You've almost made it," she called out.

Benjamin looked up. Jennifer could see that his face was very pale. Another thunder crash overhead made him grip the rungs tighter than ever. His eyes turned to the floor far below.

"No, don't!" Jennifer warned him. "That's the very worst thing you can do. I should know because I was scared of heights once too. I remember . . . it seems like ages and ages ago, I was climbing on a rock cliff with ropes and everything and suddenly I was having so much fun I forgot all about looking down."

Benjamin was nearing the top. "You have to sort of swing yourself around the ladder," Jennifer explained as she held out a hand to him from the other side.

"Thank you. I'm sorry that my hand is shaking so. I hate it because Thom is forever teasing me about being scared of heights. By the way, where is she?"

"Over there." Jennifer pointed to a mound in the hay. "But don't be nervous, she's not watching you. She is much too busy worrying about the lightning to think of anything else."

A voice quavered from the mound, "Josephine says storms are simply God moving furniture around in heaven. Of course I don't believe such childish stuff, but . . . "

Jennifer found the storm exhilarating, as if it were clearing away the oppressive air and the confused thoughts swarming around inside her own head. She could feel old memories stirring, struggling to escape. She wanted to shout her feelings out to the whole world.

"Perhaps you could tell me about climbing sometime,"

Benjamin suggested. "I've read a great deal about the Alps, especially the Matterhorn."

"If I can remember," Jennifer said, more to herself than to Benjamin. But for some reason she felt confident.

Suddenly Thomasina burst forth from the mound of hay. "It's all still. Listen!"

The storm had passed and outside the sun was shining down upon a changed world. As they walked home the sun was burning on their necks and gradually ripening the hay in the fields.

How long had they been inside that barn, Jennifer wondered. It had seemed like only a few moments and yet outside summer had truly arrived.

10
Marooned

"It's too hot for doing anything, especially cutting firewood," Benjamin complained as he dropped his axe and
flopped down on the grass outside the woodshed.

Thomasina was sitting under an apple tree nearby, husk-
ing corn.

"Where's Jennifer gone?" Benjamin asked.

"Inside, helping Josephine clean the oil lamps. I heard
them a minute ago arguing about sun bonnets. Jennifer
said her hat was so tight it was making her go bald and
then Josephine said if you don't wear it you will turn a
horrid brown colour and go all wrinkled."

"So what did Jennifer say to that?"

"Brown skin is a hundred times healthier and it looks
better too!"

"Same old Jennifer . . . "

"No, Benjamin, you're dead wrong." Thom's expression had turned serious. "It's not the same old Jennifer at
all. Perhaps she talks in the same manner, uses the same
words, but her heart isn't in what she is saying. You've
noticed surely how she is forever daydreaming or staring
out the window. And how many times does she start a
sentence without finishing? I tell you, Benjamin, we ought
to be doing something right this moment about her returning home instead of always saying tomorrow . . . tomorrow . . . Without our help she is completely at the mercy
of . . . "

"Oh don't start talking about that old photographer again.

I've heard enough about him. If you ask me it's mighty strange that you keep seeing him and no one else does."

"Go ahead—don't listen to me!" Thom fumed. "Just because you want her to stay, you're happy to sit back and do nothing . . . "

"Who said that!" Benjamin flashed back. "I'm only trying to be sensible and not let my imagination run away with me."

"Sensible . . . ha! Look Benjamin, from the bits and pieces Jennifer has told me and from what I already know, I think our time is running out. Do you realize that she has been with us almost a year?"

"Almost a year," Benjamin whistled softly, "and it seems like a minute."

"So you know what I've gone and done?" Thomasina hesitated, gathering her courage. "I wrote to Grandfather and Grandmother asking them if we could come to visit them in Toronto. I used the Exhibition as an excuse, saying it would be the best time to show Jennifer around. Mother and Father don't know yet . . . "

Benjamin whistled again. "I don't know what you are up to Thomasina, apart from getting yourself in trouble."

"We can't sit around here twiddling our thumbs while the danger to Jennifer and possibly ourselves grows worse. I'm hoping that seeing the city again, even if it is different, will jog her memory; otherwise we are in real trouble." Thom's voice sank to a whisper. "Then only Mr. Blackwood is left. He must know the way back, Benjamin. And going through him is a risk we may have to take."

"Oh him again! And what makes you think they will let us travel alone to the city, Thom? They never have before. Always Josephine or someone else has come along."

"Why not? We are perfectly responsible at our age and if Grandfather meets us at the Union Station . . . "

"Sssh—watch out, Thom. Here comes Josephine."

Jennifer was walking behind her, carrying the wicker picnic basket on one arm.

"Jennifer and I have packed a picnic lunch," Josephine announced. "The three of you may go to the lake this afternoon. But remember, no going beyond your depth and no swimming for at least two hours after lunch or you'll make yourselves sick. Stomachs need a little peace and quiet like everything else . . . "

"Did you pack any pickles, those nice, crunchy ones?" Thom asked.

"Curiosity killed the cat," Josephine snapped back with a self-satisfied smile on her face. She waved good-bye to them from the kitchen door.

"What put her in such a good mood?" Thomasina asked. "I thought you two were quarelling."

"Not seriously. Her bark is worse than her bite," Jennifer replied, tickled that she had actually been able to remember one of Josephine's sayings. "Besides she wants to get rid of us so she can clean the kitchen in peace."

The afternoon sun grew steadily hotter as the three of them trudged along the track towards the lake. Jennifer turned around once or twice to see how far they had come, but all the familiar landmarks near town had been left far behind. Except for the steady whir of cicadas hidden deep in the trees or the occasional complaint from one or the other, "I knew we ought to have hitched Old Belle to the buggy . . . we should have started earlier . . . ," it was quiet.

"I can smell the coolness from the lake," Thom shouted suddenly, breaking into a run. "Last one into the water is a big, fat P-I-G!"

Jennifer started to unroll the bundle that Josephine had handed her before leaving the house. Out of the unravelling mess a skirt appeared, then a blouse-like thing, followed by black stockings and a kerchief. Was this a bathing suit? Jennifer stared at the pile, wondering where to start, wondering why she felt so confused. But then Thomasina appeared from the bushes in a similar costume, followed close behind by Benjamin, all arms and legs sticking out from Father's cast-off winter woollens.

"Pig, pig!" the two chanted from the coolness of the lake.

"Darn stockings!" The miserable things were already coiling around Jennifer's knees as she dashed into the water. For a while Jennifer lay flat on her back, buoyed up by the billowing folds of her bathing suit. The deep blue of a midsummer day stared down on her. I seem to remember having trouble floating once because I'm so skinny, she thought, but not in a suit like this. I feel like a balloon. She tried to wriggle herself downwards and only succeeded in swallowing a mouthful of water. When was that other time . . . where?

Thomasina came floating towards her, feet stretched out like battleships. The feet struck one of the gigantic bubbles caught in Jennifer's suit and the air burped out explosively.

"Hey, Thom, swim with you to the island out there?"

Thomasina shaded her eyes as she stared at the distant clump of trees shimmering on the water. "It's pretty far . . ."

"Oh come on, Thom, the distance always looks more than it really is."

"I'm not such a great swimmer you know, Jennifer . . . oh well, I suppose it won't hurt to try."

Jennifer rolled over onto her stomach, stretching out her arms in a steady crawl stroke that pulled her far ahead of Thom. Before long though, she began to feel the drag of her swimming suit. She stopped to tread water until Thomasina had caught up.

"Whew! I wish I could swim like you, Jennifer. All I know is this silly side stroke. Say, listen to Benjamin hollering : . . "

"If you would stop splashing, Thom . . . "

Obviously alarmed at the distance the two had swum, Benjamin was running along the beach, waving his arms to attract their attention. "Come back! We're not supposed to go beyond our depth. And you remember, Thom—one of the McMurdo twins was drowned trying to swim to the island."

"Did you hear him, Thom? Maybe we should turn back. What do you think?"

"Rats to him! We've come this far and I don't feel like turning back now." Thom swung over onto her side again.

Jennifer felt caught between the two of them, but the longer she delayed, the further Thomasina drew ahead. After hesitating a few moments, she waved reassuringly at Benjamin and plunged after Thom. Strange how that island seemed to keep its distance. They must have been swimming for at least twenty minutes, yet they were still barely half way. From the deeper water below a chill arose that wrapped about their legs. Jennifer tried not to stare into the darkness that plunged endlessly away beneath them.

"Why can't Thom push it a bit faster," Jennifer thought to herself, half irritably. She turned around to her friend and started to say, "We've got to keep a move on in this cold water . . . " But Thomasina was coiled up into a ball on the surface, trying to rub one foot. "Thom—what's wrong?"

"Nothing . . . much. I'm just a little out of breath and now I have this stupid cramp in one foot. Oh golly, Jennifer, I'm scared! What if I get a stomach cramp like Mother is always warning us about?"

"Then I would rescue you. Look, I'll show you how. Roll onto your back, all right? Then I hold your head up like this while we swim along together and you try to relax. It's a cinch."

Jennifer tried to hide her own fear from Thom; how her breath was coming more rapidly now, rasping against the side of her ribs and how the awful bathing suit was weighing her down.

"I'm truly sorry, Jennifer, for pretending to be a better swimmer than I really am."

"Never mind, I egged you on in the beginning, Thom. Say, you know what? I think Benjamin is trying to launch that water-logged rowboat we found on the beach."

When Jennifer rolled over to take a better look, a wave

splashed across her face. Funny, a few minutes before it had been dead calm. Above them the solid blue of the sky had been replaced by wispy mare's tails, sure harbingers of bad weather according to Father.

"Come on, Thom, we better get moving."

"You go ahead, Jennifer. I'm just too puffed out to go any faster."

"Don't be silly. We're sticking together no matter what."

Jennifer didn't like the look in Thom's eyes, the blue-tinged lips or the spasms of trembling that were beginning to shake her whole body.

"We've got to keep swimming, Thom. Now try and kick your legs while I pull you along."

Jennifer tore off the skirt that was holding her back. As she did so, something brushed against one arm and tried to coil around an ankle. Dear angels in heaven—please not a water snake! That was more than she could handle. Jennifer forced herself to look down into the depths. "Seaweed!" she gurgled, swallowing a mouthful of water in her excitement. "And I can see the bottom now, Thom. It must be shallow the rest of the way."

Within a few minutes they were stumbling over submerged logs that reached out from the shore and then collapsing onto the sun-warmed sand of the island.

"Your brother is actually managing to row that old wreck of a boat," Jennifer observed. "I think he has reached the shallows."

While they watched, several waves broke over the bow, forcing Benjamin to drop the oars so he could bail out the water. The boat swung around and another wave caught it broadsides, smashing it against a half submerged log. Benjamin leaped out to pull her clear.

"We better give him a hand, Thom. I can practically hear what he is saying, can't you? I bet he's furious at us."

"It's no use," Benjamin called out when he caught sight of them approaching. "She was rotten to begin with and now half the side has been staved in. Looks like we are marooned for the time being."

Thomasina and Jennifer waited for the expected outburst.

"However, matters could be worse," Benjamin continued calmly. "I've salvaged your clothes from the wreck and also the picnic basket with the emergency matches, so at least we won't go cold or hungry. And no doubt someone will come looking for us when we don't show up tonight."

Jennifer watched the waves crashing against the side of the boat. Another board was dislodged and floated away. "Marooned." The word had a haunting sound if you repeated it often enough. Marooned . . . marooned . . . for an hour, a day, a week, a year . . . Time, what did it matter anyhow? And there was nothing she could do . . .

Jennifer joined the other two beside the fire which they had finally managed to get started. Thomasina had opened the picnic basket and was checking over the goodies. "Chicken pieces, watercress on slices of homemade bread, pickles . . . hurray, and look here, Josephine's cinnamon muffins."

"Thomasina, once and for all will you stop drooling over those muffins!" Benjamin banged the picnic basket shut. "We have to eat things in their proper order."

"When you are marooned on an island who cares whether you eat pickles for dessert or muffins for first course," Thomasina insisted.

"You make it sound like we are going to be here for ages," Jennifer said. "And you know it's funny but in a way I wish we were. I keep getting this terrible feeling that something is going to tear me away from you all. It's like an end-of-the-summer feeling, only worse, if you know what I mean."

"I won't let anything take you away," Benjamin blurted out. He was going to say more, but Thomasina gave him a warning look.

"How about building a shelter with some spruce boughs?" she suggested, trying to change the subject. "If it starts raining then we shall be glad of something over our heads." The three of them worked at cutting spruce branches until it was almost dark. Although the wind had died down with the arrival of evening, waves were still slapping against the shore and working away at the half-sunken boat.

"I suppose we could patch her up if we really had to," Thom remarked.

"After rowing that leaking tub all the way out here I would rather try my luck at swimming. And I'm sure they will come looking for us by tomorrow, at the very latest."

"You're probably right," Jennifer agreed. "But wouldn't it be a weird feeling if nobody knew where we were, if we just kind of disappeared into thin air as far as the rest of the world knew."

They were quiet for a long time, staring into the flames. Every so often the gum in the spruce logs would explode and send streams of sparks spiralling into the darkness. A drop or two of rain hissed into the fire.

"Why don't you two girls arrange the spruce boughs in the shelter while I build up the fire for the night," Benjamin suggested.

After he had thrown on more chunks of driftwood and the flames were licking around a mound of dry spruce branches on the top, Benjamin drew the log that he had been leaning against closer to the fire. From the shelter nearby came the sound of the girls talking and laughing as they tried to flatten the spruce boughs into a more comfortable bed. One of them gave a shriek when she rolled onto an especially sharp needle. Before long there was only the sound of the water stirring around the shoreline and farther away the cry of a night bird.

Benjamin had fallen asleep by the fire with his head resting on his knees when a branch cracked nearby, startling him awake. The fire was almost down to ashes. Another twig cracked. Was it closer this time? If some large animal was making the sound then it must have swum over in the darkness, because earlier in the day they had covered almost every inch of the island and seen no tracks. Hastily Benjamin tossed a bunch of twigs, anything he could find, onto the fire. Almost instantly flames shot up, casting a wavering light on nearby bushes. A shape darker than the surrounding night swished past the branches. It stopped on the far side of the fire. Benjamin heard a low laugh.

"Mr. Blackwood!" Without any conscious effort the words had formed themselves on Benjamin's lips.

"Aah, good . . . very good, he recognizes me at last. How quaint, the older brother keeping watch over his helpless charges—the shepherd and his sheep one might almost say. And here I was thinking that the three of them would be sound asleep after the day's little escapades. Tch, tch! Now I wonder if that wayward child still finds you so boring? Not that it matters now, for I shall soon be ridding you of your most troublesome charge. The ever-changing year runs it course and your time as well as hers is almost up." Speaking in a monotone, he began moving around the fire towards Benjamin.

"Don't listen to his words, Benjamin." Thomasina had crept from the shelter and was shaking her brother by the shoulders, trying to jolt him out of his half hypnotic state. "They are lies, lies . . ."

"So there are two of you now. But she will not wake," Mr. Blackwood whispered, pointing towards the shelter where Jennifer was lying. "She only dreams of me when the night is at its darkest."

Benjamin had taken hold of Thom's arm and together they faced Mr. Blackwood across the fire.

"How helpless you are, like puppets in my hand," Mr. Blackwood muttered. "You are nothing more than a pair of dried-up, dusty photographs! And when the year has ended I shall claim the other child too, for she belongs in no time now, having forgotten her own. Lost in time, haa . . . haa . . . lost in time . . . " His laugh echoed across the lake.

Benjamin picked up a flaming chunk of wood from the fire and held it like a shield in front of Thom and himself.

"You're lying . . . lying! You talk as if we belong to you, as if we're not flesh and blood like everyone else. But you're wrong. We are real. We'll never let ourselves fall into your evil power. And we shall protect our friend through thick and thin. Isn't that right, Thom? Thom . . . help me, this wood is growing so heavy in my hand. Thom . . . "

Thomasina reached out her hand and with all their remaining strength the two of them thrust the flaming wood towards Mr. Blackwood. But there was nothing there!

"It is you who are nothing," Thomasina screamed out. "Do you hear me? We have discovered your secret. Without us you are nothing . . . "

A laugh echoed back from somewhere. "Lost in time . . . time . . . And it is I who have time . . . "

"He's evil . . . truly evil, now I know what Thom means," Benjamin murmured.

A scuffling noise was coming from the shelter and Jennifer emerged. "What on earth are you two doing running all over the place in the middle of the night? But I'm glad I woke up because I was having that same old rotten dream again. Hey . . . look over there, on the mainland."

A light had appeared on the far shore and it was soon joined by others, bobbing about like giant fireflies. Benjamin threw some dry spruce needles on the fire, making it flare up again. The lights stood still.

"Halloo . . . " a familiar voice hailed them from across the water. "We shall be there soon. Don't worry."

11

Time-trippers

Thomasina came running into the kitchen waving a letter in her hand and plopped it down on the table in front of Benjamin. "It's from Grandfather, in answer to my letter. Read it, Benjamin. We can go to Toronto. They want us to bring Jennifer during Exhibition time. Listen, Benjamin, this is our chance, we have to take it . . . now."

"If you would let me read the letter in peace, Thom; you keep hovering over me!" A few minutes later he handed it back. "And what if Mr. Blackwood tracks us down like he did on the island?"

"I guess that's the risk we have to take—to go along with him so we can get Jennifer home, somehow."

They were quiet together, thinking back to that night on the island.

"Well," Benjamin said finally, glancing at his pocket watch from habit, "we best get started. First we talk to Mother and Father."

Thomasina thumped him on the back, making him spill the glass of lemonade he had been drinking. "I knew you would say that!"

"Why can't you be like other girls," Benjamin grumbled, wiping the lemonade off his collar. "You are too enthusiastic, Thom."

"I have to be now," she replied seriously. "And I don't think we should say too much to Jennifer about our reasons for going. She is anxious enough already. It's just a visit. Agreed?" Thomasina held out her hand to him.

Benjamin grasped it firmly for an instant before they set off to find their mother.

She was upstairs with Jennifer doing the annual cleaning out of the sewing chest. Benjamin cleared his throat once or twice before handing over the letter. After giving her a few moments to read it he said, "It's only a five hour trip by train, Mother. I promise to look after the girls and Grandfather has written that he will meet us at the station."

Mother folded her arms and looked straight at, or was it through, Benjamin and Thomasina. "Are the two of you prepared to look after Jennifer?"

"Of course!" Thom flung back the reply without noticing the strange tone in Mother's voice.

"I do not ask the question lightly. Benjamin, you at least, may have foreseen some of the difficulties." She turned towards Jennifer. "And you, my dear one, are you prepared for a long and possibly perilous journey?"

Jennifer had been quiet up to now, watching the others talk. Both Thom and Benjamin were obviously shocked by Mother's question. So what should she say? What did Mother mean, anyway? "Naturally I'd like to go," she began, "unless you need me here for any reason."

"No . . . no Jennifer. Of course you must go. I was just thinking . . . " A worried look passed across her face. "I shall talk to Father this evening," she went on quickly. "If you leave at the end of the week there will be time for a letter to reach Toronto, telling Grandfather of your plans."

Jennifer stayed behind with Mother after the other two had gone. A chill seemed to have fallen over the room. Jennifer shivered and wondered whether she really did want to go with Thomasina and Benjamin. What was so special about a train trip to the city to visit some old exhibition? Maybe she could think up an excuse, like feeling sick or having to help with something around the house . . . but no, the other two would be counting on her. "Stop being so dumb," she told herself.

Like the time leading up to an examination, the week passed slowly, yet relentlessly. Thomasina was so jumpy when they were trying to pack their bags the evening before leaving that she drove the others half crazy.

"If you would put as much in your suitcase as on the end of your tongue," Jennifer hinted. "Groan!" she thought to herself. "I'm beginning to sound like Josephine."

Somehow the night passed. Jennifer lay awake in the morning listening first to Josephine bustling about in the kitchen and later to Father hitching up Old Belle to the buggy. The air held in its breath the first hints of coming fall days. Jennifer shivered when she stepped outside, grateful for the cardigan that Mother had thrown over her shoulders at the last moment.

As they rounded the curve onto the main road, Jennifer caught a last glimpse of Mother standing in the doorway waving her handkerchief after them. Although she had managed to swallow down most of Josephine's oatmeal porridge that morning her stomach suddenly felt very empty.

At the station Father bought their tickets and pressed some money into Benjamin's hand. Afterwards as he waved goodbye to them from the buggy he warned, "Now take good care of each other and be sure to stay together." His bushy eyebrows were jumping up and down as though he wished to say more. But suddenly Old Belle was flying back down the road towards home and her morning feed of oats.

Again Jennifer had that empty feeling. "I can hardly believe we're leaving," she said to Thom. "It's gone so quickly."

"What's gone . . . " her friend snapped back suspiciously.

"The last few days of course. But it always does just before you have to go away."

"You don't sound terribly enthusiastic about our visit."

"I don't know . . . I have this strange feeling . . . " Jennifer was staring idly down the tracks where a plume of smoke was rising in the distance. Gradually it grew taller. A few minutes later the train drew up before the station, clanging its bells and hissing steam.

"Ten minutes before she leaves." Benjamin announced.

"Thank goodness I haven't seem him yet," Thom whispered to Benjamin as she glanced around the platform. "I keep feeling we are being followed. It makes me so nervous."

"I don't think he would come on the same train. And if he did he would be wearing some disguise so we couldn't recognize him."

"Well, I would," Thom shuddered.

"All aboard," came the call. "Train departing for St. Marys, Stratford . . . final stop . . . Toronto."

Jennifer tried to entangle the place names from the singsong announcement. Some were so strangely familiar she could hardly stop herself from crying out, "I know that place". No time to think about that now—the conductor was already nagging at them. "All right you three, no loitering on the platform. If you have tickets, all aboard."

Jennifer was stooping to pick up her bag when a jet of steam hissed from the engine. Startled by the sound she dropped a parcel containing jars of gooseberry preserves for Grandmother. "Oh damn, they probably shattered."

While she lagged behind, fiddling with the wrappings, Jennifer noticed a horse and black buggy racing towards the station. A figure leapt down and caught hold of the railings on the last carriage. Jennifer scrambled on board too as the train lurched slowly forward.

"Some lucky person caught the train at the last possible moment," Jennifer remarked after she had joined the other two.

"What person . . . who are you talking about?" Thom asked.

"Oh, somebody or other who managed to jump on the last car as we were pulling away from the station."

"I thought we were the last to get on," Thom frowned.

"What did he look like? Do you remember what he was wearing?"

"Relax, Thom. I only saw him for a few seconds. Besides I wasn't planning to write a book about it."

"It's no laughing matter."

"All right, Thom. I'm sorry I laughed. But you don't need to snap my head off for nothing. Why's it so important to you?"

"It just is. I'll explain later."

"Honestly, Thom, I can hardly remember . . . He did come racing up in a black buggy, I know that much. And, wait a moment, I think he was carrying some long parcel under one arm . . . "

"Tickets, please. Kindly have your tickets ready," the conductor called down the carriage.

Jennifer rested her head on the back of the seat, staring out the window at the endless drift of smoke uncurling from the engine. When she closed her eyes there was only the steady clickety-clack, clickety-clack of the wheels, broken every so often by the whistle of the train at some lonely country crossroad. Half asleep, she overheard scraps of conversation between Thomasina and Benjamin.

"Jennifer saw him get on the train."

"What makes you so sure?"

"I was talking to her, Benjamin. I'm positive."

"But how could he find out our plans? We hardly talked to a soul."

"Either he's watching our every move or he simply knows. Oh, Benjamin, I can feel his shadow hanging over us, even now."

"Sssh, she's moving."

Listening to them talk, Jennifer felt her own sense of foreboding growing. She wished she had made some excuse to stay behind. Or were they going because of her? But I don't want to go, she felt like telling them. Almost automatically she squeezed the twenty-five cent piece tucked away inside her purse.

"How long will we be staying in Toronto?" Jennifer asked later as they were digging into the lunch Mother had packed for them.

"A few days, a week perhaps, it depends . . . Care for another of Mother's scrumptious sandwiches?"

"Thom, listen to me, please . . . depends on what?"

"What about a game of checkers?" Benjamin interrupted. "We have time for a quick game."

"You two go ahead," Thomasina replied. "I'm not in the mood for checkers."

Neither am I, Jennifer thought, as she stared out the window between moves. Why do I keep getting this terrible feeling? Maybe I am going crazy.

"Next stop—Toronto. Fifteen minutes to Union Station. All out next stop," the conductor announced.

Jennifer peered through the train window. After miles of lonely countryside the sight of houses, warehouses, factories, all crowded together was somehow reassuring. And the very name of the place echoed like a familiar tune. "Toronto . . . Toronto . . ." she repeated the name several times. That's where I come from . . . Thom said so, but why did I leave? Isn't anyone looking for me?

"I can't shut this dratted bag," Thom broke in on her thoughts. "Can you sit on it for me Jennifer?"

"Why did you have to open it in the first place?" Benjamin fumed. "Oh give the silly thing to me before we are the very last people off this train. Just when we are in a hurry Thomasina . . . there now it's shut! Grandfather has probably been waiting for ages."

They joined the crowds of people streaming towards the exit.

"This is terrible!" Thom complained after been elbowed from both sides. "Don't you feel half trampled, Jennifer?"

"I don't know, I sort of like the crowds." Jennifer was gazing all around the huge station.

"I guess you would, having lived in the city most of your life. I keep forgetting."

Jennifer swung around, a question on her lips.

"So there you are!" It was Grandfather's voice booming over the crowds. "I scarcely recognized you. Grown like a bundle of bad weeds! And you, Jennifer. I am glad to meet you at last. Well, come along. I have a carriage waiting at the front."

Outside the station a surly looking fellow standing beside on of the carriages called after them. "Ride? Takes yer in a hurry where yer wants to go."

Grandfather waved him away.

"Why did he single us out?" Thom whispered to Benjamin. "I don't like the looks of him."

"I don't know what's come over you, Thomasina. You're so suspicious of everything and everybody. He is just some poor fellow looking for business."

"I . . . I guess you are right. But just the same I'm glad we're not going with him."

Jennifer settled down in the carriage, now and again sneaking a look over at Grandfather. She felt a little over-awed by this giant of a man with the elegant clothes, deep voice and whiskers that hid most of his face.

"So you have come to visit the Exhibition with us, Jennifer," he remarked. "Have you been there before?"

Jennifer nodded her head, not really knowing what to say and hoping he wouldn't keep asking questions. Why were Thom and Benjamin staring at her? "Mind your own business!" she almost snapped out loud. She watched the two of them whispering, heads bent close together. Maybe she could look around in peace for a moment or two. If I could only recognize a street or building, she thought, suddenly panicking. I've lived here, haven't I? I must have a family, a house . . . something! Thom leaned over and patted her hand.

"St. James Cathedral over there," Grandfather's voice boomed out again.

Jennifer followed the direction of his hand and gave a little start of recognition.

"You know the building Jennifer, perhaps you have been inside?"

But it was not the inside she was picturing or even the impressive spire that towered high above the surrounding buildings. It was a familiar voice she was hearing, "Put on your best skirt for church, dear and don't forget your overshoes. The streets have turned to slush overnight . . . " And then bells calling above the wind drowned out that voice on a blustery winter day, somewhere, sometime . . .

"And I remember I was in a really foul mood," Jennifer mumbled, loud enough for Benjamin to hear.

"I'm glad you remember that!" Benjamin teased.

Jennifer grinned at him. She was glad he had broken the spell. For the moment she was with friends and that was all she wanted. King, Yonge, Church, Jarvis, the streets flicked by.

"And here," Grandfather announced, motioning to the driver to stop, "is Old City Hall. You might be interested to know, Benjamin, that . . . "

Jennifer didn't hear the rest. It was as if she had been hit by a lightning flash. "Thom," she cried, pulling her friend's arm and pointing to the steps in front of the old hall. "I've jumped down those steps. Thom . . . I have been there. Don't you understand?"

"Of course," Thomasina agreed almost too casually, "after all it is your city, Jennifer." But a second later she was poking Benjamin, "Cross your fingers. With luck she's starting to remember. And watch what you say!"

"Watch what I say," Benjamin almost choked. "You are a fine one to warn me!"

Jennifer leaned back in the carriage, too exhausted to concentrate on the talk around her. How could a place feel so familiar and yet so hauntingly different? Like a dreamplace revisited, she thought to herself. A strange tapestry of sound was being woven across everything she saw around her: the clatter of horses' hooves along the cobblestone road, the call of hawkers selling their wares, "apples—fresh snows and tom-sweets from the country," the rattle of streetcars and once the far off cry of the rag and bone man, "rags, bones, bottles to buy; rags, bones, bottles . . ."

Thomasina was tapping her on the shoulder. "We're going up Jarvis Street now. Do you remember all these beautiful mansions?"

"Huh, what was that?" Jennifer stared blankly at the tree-lined avenue along which the carriage was moving.

"At least you might try and stay awake," Thom grumbled.

"But I wasn't asleep, Thom, I was just thinking and listening and . . . " For a second she felt like crying.

Benjamin came to the rescue, "Can't you see she is too exhausted to look anymore, Thom?"

Jennifer shut her eyes. Once more an overwhelming feeling for this particular place swept over her, but the trees were gone and instead of carriages there was the roar of traffic, the honking of car horns.

"Announcing Misses Thomasina and Jennifer and Master Benjamin." They had finally arrived at Grandfather's house.

A moment later Jennifer heard footsteps, tap, tapping down the circular staircase. Grandmother was tiny and smiling and best of all she was inviting them to reach into a gigantic cookie tin. Jennifer glanced over at Thomasina. The tense look of the last few days had relaxed into the old, familiar Thom expression. Good! That made her more at ease too, in spite of feeling tired and confused. A five-hour trip by train? It seemed more like five thousand.

"Are you feeling all right?" Thom asked as they crawled into bed after a late supper.

"I suppose so."

"Sorry for being so impatient earlier."

"That's all right."

"I was nervous about the train trip."

"Me too."

"Tomorrow we have to talk about plans. Jennifer . . . ?"

"Yes?"

"I don't know why, but I feel better now we are here. You too?"

"Mostly . . . it seems sort of safer being with your grandparents."

Grandfather called goodnight to them from the landing. "Early to bed, early to rise, because tomorrow is Exhibition day."

The last thing Jennifer remembered hearing before she fell asleep was the scuffling of the lamplighter outside their window as he lit the gas lamp.

12

Promises to Keep

Grandfather stopped in front of a fountain by the entrance to the Exhibition grounds. "Now if by any mischance we become separated, we shall meet here by the fountain." He pulled out his waistcoat watch. "Five o'clock at the very latest," he warned. "That leaves ample time for dinner before the Grandstand show."

Benjamin pulled Jennifer to the edge of the fountain and pointed out the coins littering the bottom. "Let's make a wish. Here's a copper for you, Jennifer, and one for me. Ready?"

The coins broke the surface of the water, swaying like dancers before coming to rest side by side on the bottom of the pool.

"I wish," Jennifer said under her breath without pausing to think, "that no matter what else happens nothing will ever separate me from my two friends here."

"What a dumb wish," she told herself afterwards. "I could have wished for my very own horse or a hundred and one other neat things." Nobody was talking about going away. Yet she could not seem to shake the feeling of foreboding hanging over her.

"I'll tell you later what my wish was," Benjamin whispered.

"Make way for my copper." Thomasina barged up beside them.

As Jennifer watched the ripples dying away she was startled by a smiling face looking back at her. It was guarded on each side by the figure of a boy and a girl. Is that really me? she wondered. And was there another Jennifer whom she scarcely remembered fading away with the ripples, a Jennifer without these two friends, without this pretty face?

"There now!" Grandfather threw in a final copper.

Jennifer splashed some water at Thomasina and Benjamin and then ran out of reach. "Who cares?" she thought. "I'm going to have fun today and not worry about stupid things."

Grandfather was tapping his walking cane on the side of the fountain and watching her closely. "Are we all ready now, Jennifer? Do you each have the twenty-five cents from Grandmother?"

Jennifer fumbled inside her purse for the money Grandmother had given her before leaving the house. But the coin she pulled out was the twenty-five cent piece that Thom was always fussing about. Why was it so important? "Time will tell, I guess," Jennifer said quietly.

"All right," Grandfather announced. "Exhibits first, followed by a grand finale on the midway. Where shall we go first?"

"The animals," Thom piped up, "especially the work horses."

"What about the Pure Food Building?" Benjamin added.

"Excellent idea!" Grandfather chuckled. "With all the free samples there, you three won't be so liable to eat me out of house and home. Now, Jennifer, you haven't suggested anything yet . . ."

Jennifer looked around for inspiration. "Machines," she blurted out, wondering how that idea had sprung into her head.

"A fine way to end the morning," Grandfather agreed. "Off we set."

It was almost impossible to pull Thomasina away from the animal exhibits. First she had to look at each horse in turn. Then there were the cattle, the sheep, the pigs, the dogs, the geese . . . and finally one pathetic turkey with half of its tail feathers missing. "I could look after the poor thing," Thom pleaded.

"Not on your life," Benjamin declared. "I've rarely

seen such an ugly beast! Besides, Josephine would have it in the soup pot before you could say Jack Robinson."

"It's not ugly!"

"Come on, Thom," Jennifer agreed. "That turkey makes me think of food too, not that I'd want to eat *it*."

But after an hour of wandering around in the Pure Food Building with the smell of candy floss, frying sausages, fudge, fresh bread dangling before their noses, even Benjamin admitted they should move on to the machine exhibit.

"While I can still walk," sighed Grandfather who was carrying the free samples they had collected for Grandmother.

Jennifer sniffed the air at the entrance to the machine exhibit. "Smells good," she thought. "Polished metal, brass, fresh paint . . . " She watched Benjamin and Thomasina circling around a new model automobile for the year 1909.

"Isn't she beautiful?" Benjamin remarked, fingering the horn.

"Dare you to blow it!" Thomasina pretended to push down on his hand.

"You do and I shall tell Grandfather."

Thom made a face at her brother.

"Perhaps I ought to buy an automobile sometime," Grandfather mused. "More and more people are, you know."

"Could you learn how to drive it, Grandfather?" Benjamin asked.

"Certainly, I'm not that ancient, Benjamin. If you can handle a spirited horse you can handle an automobile, or so they say."

Jennifer frowned as she stood apart from the other three, listening to their chatter. What looked marvelously modern to them struck her as somehow stodgy and old-fashioned. "I don't know why," she confessed to Thomasina later as they were walking through the agricultural machinery.

"Ssh . . . we can talk about it later, Jennifer. I don't fancy Grandfather listening in."

Thom's secretive reply only added to Jennifer's confusion. She lingered behind the others, looking half heartedly at the newest haymowers, horse drawn seeders, a huge tractor with steel lugged wheels . . . Suddenly Jennifer caught sight of something that caused her to shove past the others.

"Why the sudden rush?" Thom asked.

Jennifer didn't reply. She stopped in front of a threshing machine and stared up at the rows of glistening teeth. Not a wisp of straw was hanging from them, not a speck of dust or cobweb anywhere. "The dust and noise when it's running are terrible," she said loud enough for Thom's sharp ears to hear.

"You seem to know a great deal about threshing machines, Jennifer." She glanced over at her brother.

"Of course . . . " Jennifer stopped. Why were they always staring at her? They seemed to be towering over her, shooting upwards, their voices coming from an immense distance.

Jennifer headed for the exit. "I'm getting out of this creepy place."

Thom intercepted her friend as she ran out of the exit into the bright sunshine. "Jennifer, did I say something wrong? Tell me what the trouble is."

"I . . . I just felt dizzy for a moment, that's all Thom. Everything's fine now. Look, let's go to the midway . . . okay?"

"Please don't change the subject, Jennifer. Besides we have to wait for Grandfather."

Benjamin came running up. "What's wrong?"

Thomasina motioned to him to be quiet. "Benjamin," she whispered, "I'm scared. I don't like the look on her face. What should we do?"

"Stay close together as Father warned and don't leave her alone, even for a minute."

Grandfather's voice took charge. "No talk of midway rides until we have rested up and eaten Grandmother's sandwiches." He passed a handkerchief over his forehead.

"I dislike this enervating heat. It's enough to make anyone feel strange."

Later on as they were walking towards the midway Jennifer could feel the heat of the pavement burning through her boots. "We've got too many clothes on," she grumbled to Thom. It was too hot to even think properly. "I'm not going to worry," she kept telling herself. "It's pointless . . ."

"Have you got your money ready?" Grandfather asked. "All rides for children cost five pennies. Now while you three are riding the ferris wheel, I shall rest myself on this bench here."

The girls scrambled into the first empty seat that swung around. "Lucky us!" Thom chortled. "We're stopping at the very top of the ferris wheel while they load. Won't Benjamin be envious."

They could see farmland surrounding the city and the lake disappearing over the horizon into the white heat of the sun. Although the pavement below shimmered in the heat a cooling breeze ran across their faces. Jennifer swung the seat and called down to Benjamin. "We've been up here for ages."

Slowly the ferris wheel gained momentum again, swinging them from one world to another, the lake on one side, train tracks, factories, then houses on the other, until finally it began to slow down. Jennifer was the first to jump off.

"I saw the most perfect thing when we were coming down," she called back to Thom. "I've got to find it . . . "

"Jennifer, wait . . . What are you talking about?"

"Don't worry Thom. I'll be back in a second." Jennifer dodged through the crowds, but someone blocked the way each time just as she was about to catch up to the man with the marvelous singing birds. Jennifer could see them more clearly now. Whenever the man twirled the sticks to which the birds were attached, they whistled and flung out their wings. They were so beautiful.

Suddenly the man wheeled around. A cap was pulled low on his forehead hiding half his face. "I knew someone

130

was following me. You're after one of my singing birds, I suppose?"

"Oh yes," Jennifer gasped, completely out of breath.

"Well they don't come cheaply now-a-days."

"I have five cents." Jennifer held out the money.

"Not nearly enough." The man spat on the ground and turned as if to leave.

"No . . . don't go, please. How much does a bird cost?" She fumbled around in her purse, finally pulling out the special quarter. "Will this do?"

He flipped the coin in his hand. "Ah, this is indeed a rare coin my dear child and I am a collector of the unusual. In return I shall give you one of my priceless singing birds."

Although there was something about the man that frightened Jennifer, she reached out her hand to take the shining bird with golden wings.

At that instant Thomasina ran up. "Don't take the bird," she gasped. "It's a trap." She wrenched the stick from Jennifer's hand and in doing so broke it into two pieces.

"Thom, how could you!" Jennifer was close to tears she was so angry.

"And how could you be so careless . . . surely you remember the fortune teller at the circus?"

"Thom, you don't mean it's the same person? But I gave him my coin."

"Jennifer . . . you didn't!"

Benjamin hurried up. "What's the fine idea of running off like that, you two? I thought we agreed to stay together." Something in Thomasina's face stopped him short.

"It was him," she hissed. "Mr. Blackwood . . . And he tricked Jennifer into giving him the twenty-five cent piece."

Benjamin spun around. "Where is he now?"

"I've lost track of him."

"No, there he is!" Jennifer pointed to the bird man who was hurrying off through the crowds.

"Come on," Benjamin said, grabbing Jennifer's hand. "We've got to follow him."

Thomasina's face was white. "It's a risk we have to take."

Jennifer could feel Benjamin's hand shaking. Maybe that coin really was important, she thought. "It's your last link." Those were Thom's very own words. Last link with what? With the strange, confused memory stirrings of the last few days? "What stupid thing have I done!" Jennifer's own heart was pounding as they chased after the bird man.

"Don't follow too closely," Benjamin cautioned. "He mustn't see us."

"But he knows we are following," Thom insisted, "and what if it's a trap?"

"Remember what you once said, Thom? Going through him is a risk we may have to take if we want to get Jennifer back. I remember your exact words because at the time I thought they were silly."

"Going through him . . . " Jennifer echoed the words. Something in them strengthened her resolve to confront this bird man whoever, whatever he might be. She caught a glimpse of him ahead, weaving through the crowds, his birds swirling after him. "He's veering off from the midway," Jennifer panted, stopping for a moment to catch her breath.

As the crowds thinned out it became more difficult to hide. Suddenly he swung around and stared at them.

"I wish Grandfather was with us," Jennifer whispered.

"Perhaps he is already looking for us," Benjamin said.

The bird man turned and disappeared into one of the buildings.

"We'll fool him by going around to the other entrance," Benjamin suggested.

"I think Thom is right—he's trying to trap us," Jennifer said, as they slipped through the back entrance. She hesitated for a moment when she saw the machines, then plunged after the others. Where were the crowds of people and why was the light so dim? The place looked practically deserted.

"Welcome, my dear children," a voice echoed from

behind one of the machines. "I have been waiting for you. How clever you were to come by the back way."

"Mr. Blackwood!" Jennifer breathed the words out softly.

"Ah, the child remembers my name at last. How convenient that you fell into my clutches when you did. I needed someone like you to prove my mastery over time. And was it not a splendid year I gave you? However, I am afraid it is all over my dear child. You see, I hold your only connection to the real world . . . " The twenty-five cent piece shone in the dim light as he tossed it from one hand to the other.

"It's hers. Give it back, you thief," Benjamin yelled, moving towards him.

"How dare you defy me? You who are mere servants, tools in my hand . . . After all, my dear boy," he added mockingly, "it was you who kept her here."

"We never did!" Thomasina shouted. "We're friends and we would lay down our lives for her, something you could never understand."

"Enough!" Mr. Blackwood thundered. "You are nothing but wasted photographs in my hands."

Thomasina and Benjamin fell back and slumped against the wall.

"And now, child, you will shortly be joining the others . . . forever." Mr. Blackwood moved towards her. "However, I must take one last photograph before my power is complete. Then my camera and I shall be masters of time . . . time . . . time . . . " His laughter reverberated around the exhibit hall.

Once more Jennifer felt herself being sucked down by the weight of those words and the dark shadow of Mr. Blackwood's cloak. She managed to twist herself around so she was facing Thom and Benjamin who were still crumpled against the wall.

"Cloak," Thom stuttered. "Try . . . "

Jennifer understood. With all her remaining power, she lunged towards the cloak, hurling it back into Mr. Blackwood's face. The camera crashed to the floor and there, lying below it, shining like the golden bird itself, was her twenty-five cent piece! Jennifer snatched it up and ran back to the others.

"What . . . what happened?" Benjamin asked. "Has he gone?"

Jennifer helped them up. "Hurry," she pleaded. "We don't have much time."

A low laugh followed her. "It's no use hurrying. Look! They are like old photographs now, beginning to fade and crack."

Jennifer tried to shut the voice out.

"Why not abandon them and escape yourself?" the voice coaxed her.

Jennifer pushed her friends ahead. They felt oddly light and fragile. "Thomasina, Benjamin . . . please. We've got to find a way, all of us, together."

"No way now," the voice called after them, "you are lost in time . . ."

"But I don't see any door," Thom said faintly.

"Let's sit down and rest," Benjamin pleaded.

"No . . . keep going." Jennifer was pulling them towards the threshing machine. "We can rest in my hiding place," she promised. And maybe, if she remembered everything right, there was a chance . . . Sliding aside a panel in the belly of the machine, she pushed the others inside. "Don't listen to Mr. Blackwood," she ordered. "And don't let go of my hands."

"Are we going home?" Thom asked. "Oh Jennifer, I'm so very tired."

Mr. Blackwood's voice swept all around them. "It's no use . . . you can never escape me."

Louder and louder the voice rose, like the roaring of a vast wind. There was no way Jennifer could shut it out. Thom and Benjamin's hands felt dry and papery as if they would crumble in her grasp. She wanted to scream, to let go . . . Suddenly the noise faded away and they were tumbling effortlessly through space.

"There's not much time left," Thom was saying. She pressed Jennifer's hand with her old warm, strong grip.

"I can see Grandfather's house already. And if you look just a tiny bit farther, around the corner . . . ".

Jennifer strained to see. "Why it's . . . yes, it is my house, Thom. I can see the lilacs, the white picket fence . . . everything!"

"Don't try to follow us," Thom warned. "Now it's your turn to trust us. And remember to look for Grandfather's house when you get back."

Benjamin was thrusting a sticky lozenge into her hand. "I hope you will read it when you get back," he said shyly.

"Goodbye, Jennifer, goodbye." Their voices were all around her now. "And don't forget . . . promises to keep . . ."

A bright light shone into Jennifer's eyes as she struggled to get up. "A flashlight?"

"Sure is kid," the museum guard replied, "and for a moment there I thought you were hurt really bad. Guess you fell from that machine, eh? Crazy fool kid! Why didn't you stop when I called out? And then with the power being cut off in here and everything . . . Aren't exactly talkative, are you? Well, I put through a call on the P.A. system and your parents will be along any minute now."

"Mom . . . Dad . . . " It would be so great to see them again. It seemed like ages. Jennifer leaned back against the wheel of the threshing machine and shut her eyes for a moment. The lozenge was still in her hand stuck fast to the twenty-five cent piece. "Just give me a second," she whispered, "and I'll read the message on it, Benjamin. And don't you worry, Thom, I will go looking for Grandfather's house, around the corner or wherever. I promise . . . I have all the time in the world."